Lost in Vietnam

AWOL in
Southeast Asia

LARRY CRAIG

DEDICATION

This novel is dedicated
to the people of Vietnam.

CONTENTS

ACKNOWLEDGMENTS

Photos by Vern Shibla
and narrative by Bill Ayers
have been used with permission.

Layout by Jane Myhra.

Editing and Inspiration by
Waupaca Writers Club and
Waupaca Area Library.

Mary Blocksma, a friend from
college, got me started with
Google Docs and was a tremendous
help in the early days of this project.

Lost in Vietnam

CHAPTER 1

Blood Spurts

I had already been in Vietnam way too long when Major Fleece sent me on a mission with the mechanized unit of the Twenty-fifth Infantry Division, called the Three-Quarter Cavalry, to see how the body count was shaping up. Major Fleece was the officer in charge of our newspaper, The Tropic Lighting News, as well as a friend so I couldn't say no. My best friend and constant companion was Joe Duffy. He and I hitched a ride down to the Cavalry where they were already lining up their APC's (armored personnel carriers) when we arrived. I reported to the company commander, Captain Bobby Jones. Jones told me to climb in and ride in the tank with him. I asked if Joe could come along, but Jones said there was already a reporter from the civilian press along so Joe would have to wait for another time.

Our convoy began rumbling along toward the main gate of the 25th Infantry Division's base. Since we were in the lead at this point, the dust we were stirring up didn't block my view of the prisoner of war compound that abutted the gate. Conjugal visits were allowed there.

When I was at the base a couple of weeks ago, a big friendly MP had pointed to a couple enjoying the privilege, so I gathered it was allowed mostly for the entertainment of the guards. Winning the hearts and minds of the people the military way.

We pulled up to the gate and stopped and I got a good look at about two hundred Vietnamese women lined up at the gate waiting to have their I.D. cards checked so they could go to work cleaning up the living quarters of our officers. They wore identical conical hats with strings tied under their small chins. All of them wore cheap looking *ao dais*—not much more than pajamas with a floor length scarf—pretty much the national dress for women in Vietnam.

Before long we were waved through the gate which swung out to let us pass. Soon the thirty-foot high guard tower and the concertina wire that surrounded the base faded into our dust. At ten a.m. the sun was already blazing, and I patted my canteen for reassurance.

As a combat correspondent for the Army, my job was to ask questions and write stories. As we rumbled along seated on steel benches, I told a guy named Hank Phillips that I'd like to ask him a few questions for an article I would write for the base newspaper and which would also be sent to his hometown newspaper. Nobody ever turned down the chance for a little glory and Phillips was no exception, so he proceeded to tell me that he had joined up hoping to be sent to Vietnam because his father had been a soldier in WWII and his grandfather the same in WWI. He said that he believed in the war at first, but because of things he had seen he was not so sure anymore.

I said, "What kind of things?" He fidgeted with the M60 machine gun that he was holding barrel straight up between his legs and mumbled, "Oh the usual like everyone else I know."

"Had you considered going to college?" I asked.

"Sure, I had straight A's in algebra, geometry and trig. The school guidance counselor wanted me to apply to a top-notch school."

"Why didn't you?"

"It wouldn't have mattered. Dad works in a body repair shop with no benefits. To take the family on a fishing trip to Minnesota two years ago he had to work seventy hours a week for a month before we went and the same when we got back from the special week of camping and fishing. He's a wonderful father. He would have been ruined if I had needed money for college. None of my friends went either so it was all right."

At the nearby village of Cu Chi, we could have turned left and followed a bus to Saigon or right toward Tay Ninh. We took a right and enjoyed the smooth blacktop Highway 22 for about thirty clicks.

I took notes while talking to Private First-Class Roger Runson. When I asked him about alternatives to the military he laughed and said, "I quit school as soon as I turned sixteen and couldn't wait to sign the papers when the recruiter showed up at the National Guard Armory. He said that I would get a signing bonus if I joined and would be able to choose my training. What a joke that was. The bonus never materialized and the only training available was boot camp and advanced infantry training. Dad died two years ago in a coal mine accident and Mom was stuck with three kids. I needed to get out of the house and send home some money. The military was there asking for me, so I took the easy way out and joined."

The kilometers clicked by.

We then took another right and headed into the Khoi Trung Forest which was dry and easy to penetrate with our mechanized tracked vehicles. About fifty yards in, Captain Jones raised an arm and the column came to a noisy stop. Jones was about 6'2, stood ramrod straight and was clean shaven as usual. In a severe tone that did not invite conversation he told Sergeant Hank Phillips to pass a message to the next vehicle. Phillips climbed down and slowly walked to the APC directly in front of us in the line and called up to the driver to take the lead. Sergeant Phillips was a teenager. He looked underweight under his camouflaged steel helmet about two sizes too large. Tucked into the band that held the camo in place on his helmet were matches, two cigarettes and a p38 can opener. My p38 was on the chain around my neck that also held my dog tag which fortunately never had to be read.

Philips came back up and nodded to the captain. With the sun nearing its apex we opened our canteens in unison and sipped conservatively. Private Runson rested his M-16 rifle on the rail and stood serenely attentive next to Captain Jones ready to jump at the meager winked hint of a command. I wouldn't say that he acted the obsequious sycophant, nor would I have guessed at that point that he had a mind of his own. And what was Bill Smith from the *Detroit Free Press* doing here? Most civilian journalists in Vietnam never left Saigon. They just hung around the bar on top the Rex Hotel with the Red Cross donut dollies who loved to lay by the pool tanning. These lazy reporters based their stories on the news released by the Army's Public Information Office, including the military's daily update on the progress of the war commonly referred to as the Five O'clock Follies. At this point I naively thought Bill and I might team up to write something truthful about the body count. I tried to engage him in conversation, but he only responded with a nervous grunt. He was obviously too new to the war to be able to do anything but shake in his brand-new civilian boots.

Jones seemed relaxed and serious while adjusting the strap on his helmet as he told us that the nearby village of Xa Cau Khoi was not friendly and we should expect trouble ahead. APC's fanned out to our left and right leaving us safely in the rear as the advance started.

About an hour in we were met with 50 caliber machinegun fire. We all got our heads down and I thought about how closely the round had whizzed by my helmet. It screamed like a sick cat flying over a cliff. Our radioman contacted our flanks and we were told that no one had been hit but fire had been returned with one of our own fifty caliber Brownings. Jones was no longer relaxed. He stood far forward in the tank. He was red in the face and clearly starting to boil. Our intelligence had assured him that the Vietnamese had no such weapon in the vicinity. Nothing else was said but it seemed likely that we had been fired on by our own gun. Circular firing squads were nothing new, but the incident left everyone edgy.

Jones then had the flanks stay in position as we moved forward, bringing our entire company into a straight line which now had ten armored personnel carriers spread out over forty or fifty yards with our tank in the middle. The two hundred soldiers interspersed on the ground had their M-16's, M-60's and grenade launchers at the ready. We were in the lead. Runson with his M-16 and Philips with his M-60 machinegun stayed on board with Jones, Smith and me.

On this bright and shining day I had just tilted my canteen back to drink as our tank came to a sudden stop, throwing water in my face and on my new camera. The Captain pointed to a Vietnamese child lying in the grass fifteen yards in front of us. The child was face down with his arms to his sides. His hands were empty. He wore dark shorts, no shirt and rubber tire soled sandals. His back moved up and down as he breathed. Captain Bobby Jones from South Carolina was a West Point graduate class of 1963. The young captain pointed to Sergeant Phillips who still had his M60 between his legs and said, "Shoot." I watched Phillips spray about twenty rounds into the grass several feet from the child and felt a pang of relief. I had thought after talking with him that he was a good person and now I was sure of it.

The captain then said to Private Runson, who still had not lifted his M16 rifle, "Shoot the little bastard." Runson aimed carefully and fired off several rounds that came closer but still missed. In my mind I still see the child's young, beautiful brown back heaving up and down as his murder unfolded. In frustration the captain yanked the M16 from the now shaking soldier, took aim and said, "This is how you win a war," and fired five rounds into the boy. The blood splattered all over my brain forever and the little Vietnamese scout's chest was stilled except for the vivid image etched into the minds of all who witnessed it.

I should have yelled wait or stop or why or shouldn't we arrest him and interrogate him. But I was silent, as was the civilian reporter. Nobody said anything and the body count continued to rise. Call it adrenaline or just plain fear but there was no excuse for the grisly crime that we all aided and abetted. Following the killing of the boy Jones took Philips and Runson with him for a walk in the woods. They returned a few minutes later and we all turned around and backtracked towards Cu Chi. I was standing next to Runson and while Jones was busy laughing it up with Smith, I asked what they had discovered in the woods.

He sadly reported, "A few yards into the trees we came to their campsite. Like good scouts they had thrown sand on their campfire, but it was still warm— about the same as the boy's body at this point, I thought. We could see where four of them had slept around the campfire close together. The fire had been in the middle of a small clearing so they would have had a nice view of the night sky. Had they been boy scouts in the states, they would have been working on badges for astronomy. We could tell by the sleeping arrangements that none of them was much over five feet tall. The indentations in the soil around the fire made a square. A path went about thirty feet from their campsite to their latrine where they had simply tied a small log between two trees. Near their toilet we found these."

Runson took a pink handled letter opener and a small booklet from his right breast pocket. The letter opener had a one-inch round mirror at the end of the handle. Runson said "My guess is that the dead boy remembered that he had left his mother's mirror and was running back to get it when we trapped him." With tears threatening, he made sure no one was watching him before continuing, "I picture three mothers embracing their young sons as they arrive back in Xa Cau Khoi. I then picture the dead boy's mother screaming, "Where's my angel? What happened? How could you leave him? Is he all right? Is he coming behind? What was the shooting we heard?"

Runson was unable to continue. Philips eased into our conversation as we neared Cu Chi and with a nod toward Jones said, "If no one else frags that motherfucker, I'll do it myself. I hate his chickenshit guts. I'll write to his worthless bitch of a mother and tell her the world will be a better place when her soulless offspring is cold stone dead."

The captain had paid no attention to the booklet so Runson and I took it to Tuan, the company translator. He brightened up as soon as he saw it and said that it was the manual for the Ho Chi Minh Communist Youth League. He knew it well because he and all his friends had belonged.

"What does it say?"

Tuan read the following:

The Ho Chi Minh Young Pioneer Organization is an organization of Vietnamese teenagers, founded by the Communist Party of Vietnam and President Ho Chi Minh, directed by Ho Chi Minh Communist Youth Union. The Ho Chi Minh Young Pioneer Organization is an educational force in and outside school, the reserve force for the Communist Youth Union and is the pivotal force of teenage movements.

The Organization takes "Uncle Ho's 5 teachings for children" as aims for its members to practice:

1) To love Fatherland and the compatriot;

2) To study well and be hardworking;

3) To practice good solidarity and follow strict discipline;

4) To keep well hygiene;

5) To be modest truthful and brave.

Runson said, "The kid was a fucking Boy Scout and Jones killed him. We can't let the miserable maggot get away with it."

Philips said, "I'll put in my poker winnings and provide the grenade if someone else will plant it under the loser's cot."

Runson then roared enthusiastically, "I have a few hundred dollars in my footlocker and can't think of a better way to spend it. Probably every man in the company would want in on this."

Within two days of the murder of the child, $1,800 was raised. Fortunately, word got to the First Brigade commander that he was about to have Jones sent home in a body bag and Jones was transferred to Pleiku up north near the DMZ (demilitarized zone). The Brigade Commander was so thrilled to get rid of him that he never asked the first question about the money.

"Now what do we do with the money?" Phillips said.

Tuan said, "I have a cousin in the village. I could go to visit and give the money to the boy's mother."

Runson was thrilled with the plan. Tuan said he'd go that evening after work.

Tuan reported back in a couple of days that the money had been delivered to the boy's mother. "She was crying hysterically," he said, "and I could not understand what she was saying, but her husband told me that the money would be used for the school the boy had loved. A permanent display would show his smiling face along with the pink mirror and the handbook that had also been returned."

The gruesome game of body count was a startling feature of the war. General Westmoreland, our commander in Vietnam, was sending some three hundred young G.I.s home each week in body bags with dog tags in place. To justify this tragic waste of American lives, the government developed the criminally insane strategy of bragging about "enemy" killed. It became such an important part of the whole deception of the American people that by the time I arrived in Cu Chi, our company commanders had pretty much gotten the knack of it. Numbers were routinely falsified, sometimes in comical and often tragic ways.

One time after two of our guys were killed by "friendly fire" coming through some trees that separated us from the rest of our unit, I watched as the company commander had his men dig up old graves in an ancient-looking cemetery. The ground was hard and overgrown, but after a few minutes of fruitless scratching at the packed soil, the Captain declared, "Make that thirteen enemy killed." We hadn't moved enough of the soil to find even a single old bone!

While walking near a Michelin rubber plantation not long after the killing of the scout, we picked up a scrap of an old black tennis shoe that had been decomposing since about the time the French had their last match here in colonial splendor. The company commander used it to justify a body count of eleven.

Captain Jones was never officially charged for the murder of the child. He went on to win the Medal of Honor and was eventually promoted to Lieutenant General. After his military career he held high positions in our government. Fifty years later, the boy's blood would still spurt like Old Faithful in my damaged brain.

CHAPTER 2

Dumb Ass

At this point you may well be wondering how I managed to get my dumb ass to Vietnam in the first place.

After getting booted out of the Peace Corps, I got tired of dodging the draft and joined the Army. I had been in the Peace Corps the previous summer having answered the eloquent call of President John F. Kennedy. I trained at San Diego State University and in Tijuana, Mexico, for service in Peru but was deselected because the FBI turned up a discrepancy in my application—I had left an excruciating six-week stint at Northern Baptist Theological Seminary off my application. They were trying to teach me Greek and how to run a Sunday school. What I was actually looking to get out of seminary was a reason to keep my sagging faith in the biblical story.

After two years of well intentioned Peace Corps service I probably would have returned home a better Christian, ready to join the modern-day crusades of the religious right. Well, it didn't work out that way and when my mother heard upon my return from the war that I would not be going back to seminary because I no longer believed, she told me she never wanted to see me again as long as she lived. I immediately told her that I loved her, and she could not get rid of me that easily. My parents had sacrificed for four years to put me through Wheaton College on Dad's union steelworker wages. At the time I did not understand the magnitude of the investment they had made. They were devastated but eventually relented. In the end we were never estranged.

Once in the army, I went through six months of basic training and advanced infantry training at Fort Gordon, Georgia. The training was wonderful. I managed to run a five-minute mile with my boots on and hand walk the horizontal bars with ease. Shooting practice with an old M-14 rifle was a breeze.

Winter hit Georgia hard in December 1965 and made me wish I had stayed with my new black Volkswagen in Chicago where all the women seemed warm and friendly. A case of meningitis in another barracks closed the entire base for three weeks ending my training for a while. We were told to stay put but I discovered the lending library at the USO, a nonprofit charity that puts on shows and provides services for the military. This was when I finally started to read in earnest. I went through several books a week while supposedly confined to barracks.

The sun finally came back, and training resumed. Learning to shoot a 50-caliber machine gun or operate an ugly little grenade launcher didn't seem as important as catching up on my sleep. After a wonderful night of reading by the one bare bulb that was left on in the bathroom, I would break ranks at the shooting range and wander back a few yards to a welcoming ridge of bare red Georgia clay. With my face to the sun, I would sleep until the shooting stopped, then hop back on the truck for the trip back to lunch. Had I read with anything like this dedication before college maybe I wouldn't have had such a bear of a time with grades.

This training was designed to weed out the wimps who couldn't handle the discipline, intense physical conditioning and crazy screaming drill instructors. Well, one fine Saturday morning near the end of training, my friend Larry from Fort Wayne, Indiana and I beat the system right into that Georgia clay. Two adorable young women pulled up in front of our barracks in a big red Buick convertible. We chatted a bit then agreed to ask for some time off to go to town with them. Since no training was planned, the drill instructor bought our story and let us go with "our sisters who had driven from Indiana to see us." Whoever they were, they took us to their motel in the flashy car with Georgia plates and teased us crazy but passed on the opportunity to improve the local gene pool. As I walked down the hallway sporting the sad bulge of disappointment, the maid recognized my plight and took me into an empty room.

I had planned to go on to Officer Candidate School at Fort Benning, Georgia, but was already sure I would be going to the war regardless of my rank. I dropped the program that would have very likely put me out in the jungle as a disposable second lieutenant.

CHAPTER 3

Lucky

When training finally ended, like magic our orders for Vietnam arrived with the gift of a two-week leave. Larry from Fort Wayne and I spent some time at our parents' places, then took a job driving a big fast Oldsmobile to Florida. I set the cruise control at 70 mph and thought we made fine time for my eight-hour shift. The other Larry took over just south of Chattanooga and I slept peacefully until a Georgia State trooper pulled us over for speeding. I heard the cop tell Larry that the whole force had been trying to catch us for an hour. He had us follow him off the interstate to a quiet little town where he woke up a justice of the peace and left us in his custody. The trooper went his merry way assuming we would be lucky to pay a $200 fine. We felt lucky in another way. We showed our orders for Vietnam to the Justice and when told it was pay up or go down the hall to the lock up, we said we hadn't eaten and asked what he would be serving. He was pissed and told us "Pay the fine and get out!" We cheerfully said we'd rather enjoy his southern hospitality than go to war. He angrily tore up the speeding ticket then gave us directions back to the highway with a friendly warning to keep it under 80 mph. Back on the interstate Larry cranked it all the way up to well over 100mph again and before long we were at the Florida welcome station waiting for our free orange juice.

April 15th and the end of my two-week leave rolled around soon enough and I caught my flight to San Francisco where I waited around for a few days for a flight to Saigon. The wait gave me a nice taste of the future. I managed to get over the Bay Bridge every day for sightseeing in San Francisco. Soon enough a World Airways jet took me and about three hundred other scared shitless soldiers to Hawaii. I walked around the airport in Honolulu to be sure I could brag to my mother about having been there. From Hawaii we flew to Guam where we had a short stop for refueling. The next stop was Vietnam. Everybody off and watch your step!

CHAPTER 4

Yes, I Can Type

The ride in a huge Chinook helicopter from Saigon to my assigned unit was frightening. I sat staring out the open doorway expecting to be shot. The short scary ride ended, and I was in Cu Chi which is about 30 miles North of Saigon on the road to Tay Ninh. This was the Vietnam headquarters of the 12,000-man 25th Infantry Division. I spent a nervous night in the arrivals tent. I was supposed to have green camo underwear but sat on my cot in a pure white cotton t-shirt worrying that I would be an irresistible target for some sniper zeroing in on me.

Now a private first class in the Army with an 11B military occupation specialty (MOS), I expected to be sent to one of the combat units since the MOS showed that I had trained for the infantry, but I got real lucky.

In the morning I managed to find my way to the headquarters mess hall and had some breakfast. I was directed to a nearby tent where there were already several guys in front of me waiting in line to get their assignments. I finally walked up three steps to an office in a big tent and was seated at a small desk. The clerk greeted me, glanced at my paperwork and noticed that I had graduated from college. Since most of the new arrivals were just 18 or 19 years old, that was unusual. He asked if I could type and I said, "Yes!"

That YES was the magic word that probably saved my life. I was assigned to type letters home to grieving parents for the Adjutant General. He was the chief administrative officer of the division and reported to Division Commander General Weyand's chief of staff. He was referred to as the G-1 except when someone was told to rewrite a letter for the third or fourth time. No white out or mistakes were allowed.

After two months of the typing job from hell, I was talking to a sweet, mousy kid named Randy from the 2/14 who told me that he would be going back to the States soon and I should apply for his job as chaplain's assistant. I jumped at it. I rode with him back to the 2/14 and he introduced me to Major Griffith, the chaplain. The interview went well, and I was hired with a head full of plans to put my college training to use.

Randy drove me back up to Headquarters Company and waited while I loaded my duffle bag and shouldered my M-16. My next cot was in the medic's tent, still in Cu Chi, where I soon became acquainted with the cigar chomping medic, Tim.

The first morning I reported to work full of enthusiasm but was soon slapped with the reality of the work the chaplain had in mind for me. He had his own private tent, or hooch, complete with a desk and two chairs for meeting with soldiers in need. He handed me a five-gallon water can and told me to go to the pump and fill it and put it back by his private sink. Without thinking, or perhaps thinking quickly, I said, "It would be illegal for me to work as your valet."

He then sat me down at the desk for some serious counseling. He described other duties such as driving him around the base, getting his laundry done and making his bed in the morning. He asked if I was still sure I wanted the job. I said "No," and suggested I go find another job. He did not seem to want to tell anyone I had been fired for not wanting to be his valet, so there I was, not yet lost but definitely unemployed in Vietnam!

I took the employment search seriously and hopped on a deuce-and-a-half—that's military lingo for a two-and-a-half ton truck—that was part of a convoy going to Ben Luc twenty miles south of Saigon. I had arranged in advance to get off in Saigon, which I did for my interview with the folks at Mac V (Military Assistance Command Vietnam). I had called ahead and went straight to the Public Information Office at 137 Pasteur Street. The lieutenant colonel (referred to as a light colonel) I talked to said, "Sure, get the papers signed and sent here to my attention and we'll put you to work." The chaplain was happy to hear I had found a job and drew up and signed the transfer papers. The first Brigade brass signed off as well.

A few days later, however, headquarters rejected my request with a note that said the 25th was begging MACV for reinforcements, so with my 11B MOS I was not leaving. I was disappointed that I wouldn't be moving to Saigon, but, on the bright side, I was still unemployed! Two days later the 2/14 was moved to a camp near Tan

Son Nhut airfield and I tagged along with the friendly medics.

After two or three days of hanging around the edge of the airport for no good reason as far as any of us could tell, my new friend Tim and I requested eight-hour passes. Captain Blinkins handed the precious little papers to us with a clear look of envy in his pale blue eyes. He assumed we knew what we were doing. Just like that we were in a beat-out blue and yellow Peugeot taxi on our way to the excitement of the city. That we were doing this in the midst of the most infamous war of the second half of the 20th century didn't occur to us.

This was when my language lessons began in earnest. We had heard that the girls serving Saigon Tea on Tu Do Street would welcome us with open arms and loose bras so with a few Vietnamese words and some hand signals we asked our driver to take us there. The ride through the Chinese district, Cholon, was slow and mesmerizing. We were barely able to take it all in. Open sewers, pigs, chickens, old women tending naked children and small cooking fires as well as a big loose blue-gray water buffalo with long horns that would scare any sane matador blessed our vision. The enchanting smell of joss sticks burning in small temples to assist recently departed relatives on the journey to the next life added to the exotic thrill.

Once the taxi dropped us off, Tim was happy to stay with the mini-skirted hostesses, but I was too self-righteous for that common fare and started off on my own walking tour of the city. I lingered at a four-foot wide doorway where an old woman tended a fire while a young mother inside nursed her baby. The colors in the morning sun were riveting but I wandered on looking for the Cathedral. I had heard that it was called the Saigon

Notre-Dame Cathedral Basilica. I knew it would be hard to miss since it had two towers topped with large crosses reaching over 200 feet towards heaven. Soon I was in the sacristy and was so impressed that I almost said a prayer. Since the 10 percent of the population who supported the Americans and had also been the ones to collaborate with the French were Catholic, I should not have been surprised by the impressive structure and thriving congregation in the heart of the collaborators' citadel. At that point so early in my tour I was still operating on the philosophy delivered by John Wayne in the hit Hollywood movie *The Green Berets,* which had convinced me to enlist to save the Vietnamese from "Godless Communism." So just where were all the Buddhists? I soon learned they were out in the boonies kicking the shit out of my fellow GI's.

I have often wondered why nobody else seems to ponder the inevitability of John Kennedy our first Catholic president starting this war in support of the Catholic minority in this clearly Buddhist country. Catholic men running against each other in the Presidential primaries of 2012 would mimic his subservience to the church with promises to take women back in time by limiting access to birth control and advocating vaginal ultrasounds and forcing women to look at pictures of the fetuses they desperately needed to have aborted. Science flies you to the moon while RELIGION FLIES YOU INTO BUILDINGS and of course encourages you to kill family planning doctors. Praise the lord eh.

My walk continued. Little old men in tiny doorways worked at little bitty fires as young mothers tended their babies and sold Marlboros and Coca Cola to the tunes of Vietnamese music that I could only describe as singsong at that point simply amazed me. I was already getting hooked. Garfield Street in Gary, Indiana, may have been home, but this was right up my alley.

CHAPTER 5

Massage No Sex

It was as I walked by the Tan Loc Hotel, which would become a home away from base for me, that I spotted the Saigon Health Club. The small print on the sign said steam bath and massage, no sex, public welcome. There didn't seem to be any Americans around to spoil my moment of cultural relativity, so I walked in. The greeting by the old woman at the front desk (my friends would have called her the mamasan) was perfunctory. In a jiffy I was showered and flat out on a table covered with a crisp clean white sheet.

The table was hard, and the therapist Bo Nam pummeled me relentlessly. She appeared to be thirteen or fourteen years old and was sweet and cheerful. She rubbed oil into my back, butt and legs squeezing and pounding the cares of the war away. She bounded up onto the table and proceeded to walk around on my back and legs digging in with her toes where the large muscles seemed to need extra care.

Bo Nam got a little careless with her toes in my crotch and by the time she sat down straddling my leg I was already getting uncomfortable in a pleasant sort of way as the blood rushed in. When she asked me to turn over, I hesitated because of my aroused condition but she just laughed and rolled me over. She pointed at my obviously ready member and said, "What's that?" with a wonderful warm and friendly smile. She then worked around the most sensitive areas with tender caresses and even blew some kisses. Fancy club or not I was ready for more of this. I asked her to massage the part that was begging for attention. She said, "Me no can do, friend Tam Muy do."

Her friend in the next booth was older and cheerfully came to the rescue. Tam Muy was no more than seventeen or eighteen. She quickly sized up the situation and went to work while on the table between my legs. As she leaned over to kiss my forehead, I unbuttoned her silky blouse and welcomed a delightful pair of royal queens into the fine morning sunlight. My heartfelt kissing, nibbling and gentle sucking prompted her to say suck harder so naturally I did. She rubbed her hard nipples along my young chest as she tongued her way to her chosen target. Bo Nam, who was obviously just learning the finer points of "massage no sex" placed my free hand on her sweet little ass and gently cradled my rapidly constricting scrotum as I looked out the wide open window at a sky that had never before seemed so blue. Two teenagers at once! Wow, what a war. A few pure white fluffy cumulus clouds left over from the earlier showers marched by like eighteen-year-old virgins flying off to Vietnam to save the world. When the volcano erupted with three months' worth of youthful enthusiasm, Bo Nam jumped up and down and giggled like the girls back in Gary when I attempted to lead them in singing "What a friend we have in Jesus all our sins and griefs to bear, what a privilege to carry everything to god in prayer." Good grief! I sure wasn't missing home much anymore.

CHAPTER 6

The Big Fat Zero

This wonderful unemployed-at-war limbo of course had to end. Soon after our unit returned to base in Cu Chi, the chaplain told me to report to First Brigade HQ for my new assignment. So, I said goodbye to my friends in the medic's tent and moved my meagre personal effects to a tent housing twenty grunts at First Brigade Headquarters. My new boss was Private Joe Duffy. He had been busted for insubordination but kept his job as brigade photographer because he was so good at it.

Joe's route to the First Brigade was amazing. He had joined the army with the assumption that what the recruiter promised would become reality. He was assigned to the 21st U. S. Army Signal Brigade at Fort Detrick in Frederick, Maryland. After suffering through several weeks of training, he decided against continuing with the Signal Corps. He was training to translate intercepted Soviet messages that were sent with Morse Code. The test that he needed to pass to continue down this mistakenly chosen career path was easy. The Army didn't want to lose any of their young geniuses who had already scored high on the Army's version of the I.Q. test. Joe got a big fat zero. He was busted from an E 2 to an E 1 because it was obvious that he knew all the answers, or he couldn't have gotten them all wrong on the multiple choice test. For punishment along with the pay cut he was sent to Hawaii!

The 25th Infantry Division was then stationed in Hawaii and Joe got there just in time to start packing for Vietnam. It was soon learned that he was a photographer and was accustomed to developing his own black and white film. He got the job of 1st Brigade photographer and was told to pack a conex. A container made of steel that was eight feet wide, eight feet high and ten feet long. Joe had two days to fill it with the supplies he would need to run a lab when he got to Cu Chi, Vietnam. After packing all the equipment and chemicals he would need, he slipped in a mattress late at night. The mattress made a lot of guys jealous when he placed it on his cot in Cu Chi a few weeks later. Joe set me up with a camera but said that the plan was to work together, with him taking the photos and me writing the stories. Our team effort paid off. The Brigade got the publicity it wanted, and nobody bothered us.

CHAPTER 7

The Striking Blonde

While working for Joe, I was sent on a convoy headed for Ben Luc, but I hopped off in Saigon and spent a nice weekend there with a German girlfriend who worked on a German hospital ship docked in the Saigon River. I had pretty much been picked up by Suzie on an earlier trip to Saigon. I had been sitting alone in the wonderful open-air bar at the Continental Hotel reading Graham Greene's antiwar novel, *The Quiet American*, when I noticed her looking at me. Maybe I was slow but at least I was smart enough to walk to her table and ask to join her.

This time I was walking down a beautiful dipterocarp tree-lined street near the PX with this striking blonde on my arm, when I came unexpectedly face to face with my Brigade commander and his first sergeant. As the lovely Colonial-era trees helicoptered their fruits down around us, I introduced Suzie to the sergeant and the colonel. We then went blithely on our way back to the *Helgoland* where she worked as a lab technician. I caught a bus to Ben Luc, did my assigned story, and went back to Cu Chi. Had I simply called my boss and told him that I had gotten stuck in Saigon when the truck I was on headed for Ben Luc broke down, he would have been prepared when questioned by the sergeant about our unusual encounter. Having neglected to make the simple phone call, I found myself facing court martial for having been Absent Without Leave (AWOL.)

I was sent to Ben Luc where my unit was based. The time spent there pending court martial turned into a fine vacation. First the Captain, who was stuck there with me, tried to get me to fill sandbags and carry them several yards around the camp perimeter to reinforce our position. I refused, stating that would be punishment which was not allowed since I hadn't been found guilty. I did offer to do the work using a jeep that was sitting idle nearby. Instead I was put to work assisting Private E1 Ed Bishop of New Jersey who seemed more than a little crazy. His wry, sly, gap-toothed smile hinted at insanity but actually hid a superior intellect. He was determined to survive the war in style. It was soon clear to me that I had found a fine new friend.

Our job was affectionately known as shit burning (how's that for style?). We would remove the half-full half oil drums from the outhouses and replace them with empties. Then we would gather our catch from the two hundred unlucky soldiers of the 4/15 1st Brigade 25th Infantry Division in a disgusting circle and pour on the kerosene. Once lit, Ed gleefully pointed out, as the black smoke dirtied the delta sky, that our only obligation for the rest of the day was to go to the fueling station and fill the five-gallon jerry cans for the next day's festivities.

With the work finished by eight and all the promise of the morning sun above I suggested that we take a drive to Saigon. Without blinking Ed said, "Let's go" and hopped in the driver's seat and away we went. At the edge of town, he said, "Which way?"

I said, "Let me drive since I know the way."

We headed North through quaint villages that seemed to float in vast wetlands that brimmed with incredible rice crops. An old red-toothed-betel-nut chewing woman carrying heavy pails of water on a *dong hai* (pole) frowned at us showing her teeth as we sped through her sleepy village blowing dust in her face. We knew that no sane or ordinary GI would have chanced this trip without armored car accompaniment on the ground and Huey helicopter gunships above---but here we were!

Elated by the tropical wind in our faces we remembered that we hadn't checked our gas supply, but luckily we had enough. We made good time and were soon parked in front of the Saigon Health Club, which was still right there across from the Tan Loc Hotel. Ed slouched in the jeep and fired up a cigar. Happy and relaxed he pulled out his wallet and smiled at pictures of his lovely wife, Cheryl and their daughters, Leslie and Diane. He just sat in the jeep smelling of kerosene as usual while I went into the club for some wartime entertainment. Our trip back to Ben Luc was uneventful and didn't take long. We flew past a bus that was overflowing with people and animals. A child was tending a goat and guarding chickens in a cage on the roof.

While working in Ben Luc with my friend Ed I had shared a bunker with a Tex-Mex guy named Luis

Menendez. He was from the part of Texas, down around Brownsville that the gringos called the Magic Valley. He told me the Mexicans called it the Tragic Valle. Luis had trouble staying awake to babysit our 50-caliber machine gun which was trained down the road towards the highway. I thought an attack from there was certainly possible and at times seemed likely. At two one morning I had trouble waking Luis to start his guard duty shift and pulled him out of his cot, but he still did not wake up. After I dragged him around for a while, he ran off to the first sergeant to complain. I don't know what he was told but after that he was much more cooperative.

Our twelve bunkers were built with sandbags on the least desirable swampy real estate in the area and we had to share our little islands with a colony of what were probably Laotian rock rats. I was amazed every time one of these critters woke me while walking around on me sniffing. It was believed by scientists that this hairy, nocturnal, thick tailed rat had been extinct for centuries. But between 1997 and 2007 the delta which covers parts of five countries was found by the World Wildlife Fund to be home to the rock rats as well as another 1,000 or so newly discovered species. This suggests that the critters were handling Agent Orange better than my friend Blake who later died from it in 2011.

The Army didn't approve of this kind of cross species sleeping arrangement, so traps were provided. One day I returned to the bunker to find Luis shaking one of the beautiful rats in our trap. I told him if he shook it again, I would let it go. Sure enough he shook it again and I let it go with a silent farewell. That's one story that doesn't haunt me at night since the friendly rat escaped.

During these sanitation worker days in Ben Luc, I visited a woman who gladly accepted the stares of the

G.I.s for 3 or 4 dollars. I paid but had to use 2 condoms to get my reward. When I took out the first one, she threw it away in disgust thinking it had already been used. I opened the next capsule slowly. When the natural lambskin condom emerged wrinkled and well lubricated, she frowned but presented her charms to be enjoyed doggy style. As I was entertained with her swinging breasts, I thought about the opportunities I had missed as a Bible banging high school goody goody and later as a Wheaton College and Northern Baptist Theological Seminary virgin. Making up for lost time was making it easy to forget the war that raged around me.

At the same time, I was most likely helping to finance the Communists and alienating the Vietnamese men who were trying to stay loyal to the Government of South Vietnam (GSVN). With my private's pay and the extra cash, I hustled trading money, booze and cigarettes on the black market, I could spend fifty dollars on a date more easily than my counterpart in the puppet army might spend fifty cents. It was no way to win over the people, but the geniuses John Kennedy had chosen— Secretary of Defense Robert McNamara and Vice President Lyndon Johnson—didn't get bogged down in this terrible war by understanding basic human nature. A little more common sense and a lot less Harvard hubris would have saved the Vietnamese and the Americans a lot of lives. If Johnson had studied at Harvard himself, he perhaps would not have been so easily taken in.

CHAPTER 8

The Straits of Malacca

The crazy idea our clueless government had in this war was to limit the tour obligation of each G.I. to 12 months. Each recruit was promised a vacation called R & R for rest and recuperation to Thailand, Hong Kong, Taipei, Tokyo, Sydney or Kuala Lumpur. At each destination the young troops were housed in or near brothels where the sex was clean, cheap and easy. Many of the frontline soldiers in Cu Chi planned to save their trips until they were almost through with their year, but the casualties for those units were so horrendous that many (if not most) guys never made it to a single one of these exotic destinations that were used to get them to volunteer in the first place.

Having grown up believing that a bird in the hand was worth two in the bush, however, my name was always on the list to go when there were empty seats on a flight. My first trip was to Kuala Lumpur just three months into my year. I was met at the airport by a Peace Corps volunteer as I had arranged. She took me down to the beach at the Straits of Malacca on the South China Sea. We stayed with a married Peace Corps couple that had been assigned to duty at a beach resort—I still wonder what kind of connections they had! The beach was beautiful. I snorkeled for the first time and sailed a little Sunfish scattering bathers as I cut it a little close heading back to the shore. I thoroughly enjoyed the company of Sally Meroz from Pittsburgh, but she wouldn't even hold my hand!

CHAPTER 9

Beaucoup Viet Cong

At this point in my twenty-one-month military career, the company commander of the first brigade administration company finally accepted my story about being stuck in Saigon, gave up on the court martial and sent me off to another company to be the clerk. That work did not appeal to me so after a few days of sunbathing and reading Kurt Vonnegut's *Cat's Cradle* near the Cambodian border, I appealed to my friends at the division newspaper and they got me transferred to division headquarters company to work with them. If the Major who signed off on the transfer had known, then that I was going to change sides in the war and live to tell the story he would have croaked before allowing it to happen. I guess I was lucky he was a Bible banging Georgian and not especially bright.

Yes, I was back in paradise, but this time I was wearing the rank-hiding black arm band favored by the enlisted men of the Public Information Office. Captain Blinkins had moved on and I was able to work the beat as if I had never burned shit for a living! Joe had also been transferred to the newspaper at Division Headquarters. On assignment, he and I were lazily walking along the main street of Ben Luc when we first saw Muy Ba. We tossed the sugarcane sections we had been chewing and sucking for the last hour and stared in awe at the amazing young beauty. I would later learn that she was sweet sixteen but she could easily have been taken for thirteen at any bar in Chicago that I might try to slip her into. Turns out the stoop shouldered old man she was with was her father but at the time I thought he was her grandfather. We barely even noticed him.

Muy Ba and the old man had reached their destination—the pharmacy where Joe and I had been practicing our French with the owner the day before. An interesting legacy of the Colonial era was the amount of French spoken. The higher up the economic ladder people were, the more French they spoke. Everybody seemed to know that too much in French was beaucoup as in beaucoup G.I.'S or beaucoup VC depending on one's perspective.

There was something about the way she walked. A lot of our guys thought you could tell the Communists by the way they walked. Joe said Muy Ba walked like a Communist. If that was true, I already knew that she was my kind of Communist.

Viet Cong was a derogatory term used by the American military to dehumanize Communist guerillas in a successful effort to make them easier to kill without remorse. Years later many of the surviving killers were spending sleepless nights thinking about what they should have done differently. The Vietnamese fighters referred to themselves as Viet Minh, meaning Vietnamese Communists. The French who had fought them and lost to them decisively had also called them Viet Minh. I would soon find out a lot more about Muy Ba and the old man—they were not Viet Minh and they certainly were not collaborators.

Meanwhile, Joe and I sauntered off to the airfield where I had been firing a 50-caliber machine gun a few months back for practice. The commander of all U.S. forces in Vietnam was General William Westmoreland and he was due in soon to review our operation. The Viet Minh were thought to be building up their forces in this part of the Mekong Delta near Saigon and the situation was considered precarious.

After our photo op with the general, we wandered back to town talking about the enchanting Muy Ba and trying to decide when to return to division headquarters at Cu Chi to turn in our stories and photos. We walked past a fishpond which boasted a regular Indiana-style outhouse perched precariously over it at the end of a narrow plank. People would regularly walk the plank, close the door and feed the fish, a much speedier way of recycling waste than the septic tanks I was used to back home and certainly better than the sky-messing oil-burning method the Army used. I soon discovered that the fish also liked the fare I sent down. Down by the river, a tributary of the Mekong, we saw another toilet poised to service the river fish. It didn't seem like the best way to keep the river safe for swimming but in a few weeks Joe and I ended up enjoying a refreshing swim there with some exuberant local kids. I don't know if that swim did it but I got a serious case of diarrhea and was confined to a hospital bed for a week. I happened to have a copy of Leo Tolstoy's masterpiece *War and Peace* with me which I read from cover to cover that week while sticking to the doctor's orders to drink a six-pack of beer a day. Tolstoy's description of a commanding general looking over his army from a place high above the valley they were in and planning their movements has stayed with me.

While strolling around town that same day Joe and I stopped to admire a young woman who was on her knees weeding a vegetable garden beside the road. We meant no harm but as we watched her breasts sway in her flimsy blouse as she worked, a man came running from the house in shorts without a shirt or shoes. He had a muscular build and stern look as he emphatically motioned for us to get moving. We were embarrassed and also relieved he didn't have his AK 47 with him. He certainly could have shot us as we fled looking stupid with our M16 automatic rifles hanging over our shoulders. Joe said as we scurried along, "That guy sure carried himself like a Communist." He didn't have to tell me. We worked regularly with translators from the Army of the Republic of Vietnam (ARVN) who would leave our base walking cheerfully back to their wives holding hands and none of them looked anything like this impressive home front defender. We naturally showed more respect for the local women after that.

CHAPTER 10

THE PINEAPPLE BOAT

The next day, after hanging around the base for a while working on a story with some G.I.s names and impressions of Ben Luc, Joe and I headed out for another look around this pleasing Mekong Delta town. He had a favorite friend who we simply called Ba which is the Vietnamese word for woman. She had a little sidewalk café selling soup and rice. Her six- year-old daughter was always with her and Joe spent hours there trying to learn the language and just putting in his time. Ba was doing fine this perfect lazy morning and after a pleasant visit we moved on towards the river.

Downstream a few hundred yards we came to a curious looking boat known as a Chinese junque, tied to a tree at the dock. Palm fronds whispered in the breeze as two monkeys hissed overhead. The junque had been modified to carry freight on a flat deck and was loaded with what looked to us like two or three thousand pineapples. Two young men were just topping off the load as we approached. While we were admiring the long neatly stacked pineapple pyramid, a young lady came up from below deck and offered us a plate of the pineapple that was peeled and sliced. We were so busy with the treat that we didn't at first notice that the young woman was the beautiful Muy Ba we had admired near the pharmacy the day before. She was dressed simply in jeans and a tee shirt. Her perfect skin was reddish brown. I almost choked as she looked up at me and asked, "Do you liked the pineapple?" in not quite perfect English.

Well, of course, the pineapple was unbelievably sweet. It had been picked perfectly ripe just a few hours before at a nearby plantation. he pineapple was nothing compared to the feast my eyes were enjoying. Muy Ba was chattering away in English about how nice it was to see us again. She had noticed us on the street by the pharmacy and said she was hoping we would see more of each other.

She said, "We must leave soon but I want to talk to you some more." She told me she had been to Paris. I was shocked. Then she said she really wanted to see New York. I said I liked the idea since I hadn't been to New York or Paris. I joked, "Maybe we can go together." At that point Joe started to ease away.

"My name is Muy Ba and I was happy to meet you." She asked me if she had gotten the grammar right and I told her to use am instead of was. I then asked her to teach me something in Vietnamese.

That was more than Joe could take. He said, "Sorry guys, I have to catch the chopper back to Cu Chi and it will be leaving soon."

"Cu Chi can wait. I want to continue my language lesson."

"Yeah, I know," Joe said as he started walking back along the river.

I yelled after him, "Be sure to tell the captain I'm working on a big story."

"Be back by Friday or there's no way I can cover for you."

,

CHAPTER 11

Vietnamese History

So, there I was by the river in Ben Luc with my future wife and no idea if I would even make it through the war and have a future. At that point the old man came up from the hull of the boat, blinked at the bright light and said to Muy Ba, "We need to get downriver to Can Duoc before dark so why don't you have your friend come along?"

Holy smokes! Was I ever shocked by his question, but it was nice to know that he thought Muy Ba was my friend! Yesterday at the pharmacy he had just seemed like a stoop-shouldered old man walking his last lap. Now it was clear that he was anything but. I was also quite surprised that he spoke English to Muy Ba. "Come on, "she said, "your friend is gone anyway, and I'll bet the sleeping arrangements are better here than back at your camp."

What a bizarre situation. Right in the middle of the war I was being invited to get on this Chinese junque with strangers, who were most likely Communists, and go downriver to a town I had never heard of. Well, this seemed a lot like my chance to be a kid again, so I said "Okay, if you'll take me I'll go, but I have to be back in Ben Luc by Friday." Away we went. Not all that far from the ocean, the Gulf of Thailand, so when we untied and pushed off the current wasn't going to take us any place because the tide was coming in. I said something to Muy Ba about it and she just laughed. Then suddenly a 500 horsepower Soviet Luba diesel fired up and we began to move swiftly downstream against the incoming tide.

Muy Ba took a seat on deck and patted the seat next to her. I sat down and started to relax and enjoy the ride as palm trees and mangrove forest flew past. We made our way south through the Plain of Reeds on our way to the South China Sea.

She pointed up and said, "Look, a zebra!"

"That's a monkey, silly."

"I know, I was just teasing you." As time flew by, she told me about her father's hopes for agricultural development in the 2,500 square mile Plain of Reeds which is a massive wetland. Only inferior floating rice every seemed to grow there and attempts to drain the area failed so the wonderful wild plants and critters still have the Plain to themselves.

My curiosity got the best of me and I said "How do you know so much English? Where are you from anyway?"

For a while she just sat there looking for more zebras in the trees I suppose as the pleasant breeze raked her shiny black hair. Then she started to talk. "I grow up pretty much right in the middle of Hanoi in the old quarter near Hoan Kiem Lake. During the time of the French my father was a civil servant working in agriculture department. I had nice life. Both of my parents loved me very much and I had many friends to play with in the park across the street by the lake. Sometimes we would even see one of the huge turtles that live in the lake. People say the beautiful softshell turtles live to be 500 years old, even older than my father!

After the defeat of the French at Dien Bien Phu, my father was recruited by the new government to draft plans for the socialization of agrarian life. He was already a member of the Communist Party and believed in the work he was doing. It was very hard on the family because he traveled all over the country researching plans for a new society while before he had never been away for more than a night or two now and then. I learned from him that under the French simple farming had been ignored in favor of rubber and fruit plantations. The country was no longer self-sufficient in rice, the single most important staple in the diet."

I thought, sure a good thing for the Vietnamese that they kicked out the French!

She told me that her father had had a dream of restoring the communal lifestyle that had thrived in Vietnam for a thousand years. At this time the country tried to improve living conditions in the north and the south, but it soon became apparent the Americans planned to replace the French with a new and even crueler colonialism. His attempts to work in the south were fruitless. For the next several hours, as we sped across the Gulf of Thailand, Muy Ba did her best to teach me some important Vietnamese history. Following is pretty much what I learned from her:

In June, 1954, the Americans brought Ngo Dinh Diem back from the United States to establish a puppet government in South Vietnam. A U.S. military mission (The Special Military Mission) was established in Saigon. The U.S. National Security Council approved an "emergency program" of economic and military assistance and replaced the French advisors with American advisors to Diem. The United States gathered a number of imperialist nations and U.S. satellite nations to form SEATO, a Southeast Asian military alliance. In September 1954, South Vietnam, Laos, and Cambodia were placed under the umbrella of protection of this Southeast Asian military group.

"Wait a minute" I said with dismay. "What do you mean imperialist? How do you know all this? You are sounding like a forty-year-old college professor. "

She just laughed and continued in the same vein and I received the following history lesson:

The party Central Committee and Chairman Ho Chi Minh correctly assessed the aggressive nature of the American imperialists and closely monitored their schemes and actions. In mid-July 1954, even before the Geneva Conference had ended, Ho Chi Minh clearly stated that the U.S. is not only the enemy of the people of the world, it has now become the principal, direct enemy of the people of Vietnam, Laos and Cambodia. Uncle Ho said our policy was to concentrate our forces to oppose the American imperialists. This statement marked the dawn of a new era in the history of our

nation, the era of opposing the Americans to save our nation.

Whoa baby. This hot looking little number may have reminded me of Bo Nam back at the Saigon Health club when I first saw her, but I was now beginning to realize that Muy Ba was a whole lot more. She cared deeply about the history of her country and knew it well. At that point I didn't think she had an insincere bone in her lovely young body. Back when I was under the spell of *The Red Badge of Courage* and John Wayne's movie *The Green Berets*, I would have simply considered her the enemy. The domino talk about it being better to fight them here rather than in our own backyards seemed criminal. Now that I had been in Vietnam long enough to appreciate the people and see that America was fighting on the wrong side in brutal civil war, she put me at ease.

She brushed against me in the moonlight and suggested a walk around the deck, I followed like a smitten puppy.

All traces of the winter dry season were fast giving way to the lush beauty of the rainy season. Moon shadow black palm images danced on the calm river as we cruised along near the shore. After about two hours of cruising downstream, the captain cut the engine and we coasted into a cove that was camouflaged with tangled vines that parted easily to let us enter. The moonlight reminded me of a lovesick evening on Stormy Lake in Wisconsin up near Eagle River. That along with the alien music of the jungle and the nearness of Muy Ba robbed me of my judgment. I knew that I should jump overboard and make my way back to Ben Luc and catch the next chopper to Cu Chi. The thrill of the moment kept me from seriously considering that option.

I took her tender hand and we walked back to our seats. A smaller engine started, and we slowly made our way along a canal that took us to the hidden village of Can Duoc. It was now about 10 o'clock and I was getting tired after a long strange day. Muy Ba told me that we probably wouldn't see anyone from the village until morning so we might as well get some sleep. I was led to a hammock which was about what I had expected.

Was I tired? I sure was. Could I sleep? No! I found the hammock relaxing and the silence comforting. The others had gone to bed with their clothes on so I did the same. The nice stash of locally laundered sheets and underwear that were back in Cu Chi seemed to be laughing at me. It would have been nice to bathe, sleep on clean sheets and put on fresh underwear in the morning. I wondered what the new day would bring. I thought about home. I thought about Mom and Dad and the precious letters that had come like clockwork. Mostly though I just worried about getting back to base before anyone noticed I had been gone. I thought I had a week to work with at most. My boss, Captain Watkins, was bound to start asking questions if I got back too late. Eventually I did sleep, deep and long.

When I got up well after the sun the next morning, I found the boat deserted. I yawned and stretched a bit, then realized I was hungry and had to pee. The last food I remembered eating was the pineapple. Did these people eat without me or were they so dedicated they didn't notice the lack of food? Come to think of it, they were all quite slim. I stepped down to the pier and saw that the water was clear for a change. There were no people nearby, but the well-worn path was inviting so I started walking with the determination of a hungry soldier. I soon came to the village which looked deserted except for the friendly little puppy that greeted me. I sat down to have a chat with Spot and thoroughly enjoyed his company.

I looked into several empty doorways and yards with empty hammocks and then came to a small restaurant with an old woman serving and an equally old man sitting and sipping tea. I sat on an old Coca Cola folding chair with a maroon plastic seat at one of two tables in the thatched roof hut. I said to the woman in my very best Vietnamese, "Lamon co cho la toi mot bua diem tam nam Saigon." I had tried to say please mam bring me a breakfast of Saigon meatballs. Of course, she didn't understand me so I tried it again.

Finally after another attempt with hand signals, she smiled and said, "Xin ong, doi mot chut." (Please sir, wait a moment.) The food came quickly and went down even faster. It was a sweet rice pudding similar to one I had tried before in Saigon and rejected. That time I had managed to trade for fresh bacon and eggs even though I had practiced the request for the local dish in Vietnamese for hours. This time I just tore into it with pleasure. The tab including coffee came to twenty-five dong, about twenty cents U S. I may have been AWOL but at least I could afford to eat.

With that little adventure over, I headed back to the relative security of the boat. There was still no one about so I just looked around. About the time I picked up the boat captain's binoculars, I noticed Muy Ba upstream about 200 feet. She was bathing in a clear pool at the edge of the canal. Her pale white breasts enjoying their liberty in the bright morning sun caught me by surprise. She shifted her legs revealing a tiny patch of black hair. She put back her arms for a leisurely yawn and my mind raced back fifteen years to Indiana where I got my first job when I was eight. My older brother was tired of delivering one hundred and forty copies of the *Gary Post Tribune* every day, so he gave me Arthur Street with twenty-five customers.

I hadn't been in business for long when I happened to look up and saw Marilyn Monroe hanging there in Mr. Villalobos' bedroom in her earliest Playboy pose.

The image was a sensation back then and now I strained for a better look at Muy Bas' agreeably large, puffy dark rose nipples. She looked even better than Marilyn in a pose that was eerily similar. I had the urge to use the binoculars and my youthful sense of morality was overruled by common sense. I walked back to my hammock and lay down feeling euphoric and a little guilty for enjoying the view so much. When I was sixteen, a fifteen-year-old Baptist minister's daughter told me that a woman's body was the most beautiful thing on earth. I never accepted the invitation to see hers, but now I sure knew what she meant.

Muy Ba woke me later and suggested I take a bath in her secret pool. I didn't bother to tell her how secret it really was but followed her up the path and had a leisurely soak in the dreamy comfort of the surprise Florida Everglades like warm clear water. After my refreshing bath, I washed my underwear and relaxed on the white sandy beach.

The captain and the old man returned to the boat in the early afternoon and we headed back down the channel to the river. We still had our load of pineapples. I complained to Muy Ba that I would be in big trouble if I didn't get back soon. She jolted me by saying, "Once we get past Go Cong on the coast and into international water, I will tell you more about the trip." I was feeling more and more kidnapped and worrying less and less about it every time she talked to me. All the schooling I had suffered or slept through at Fort Gordon, Georgia was going right down the drain. It was clear that I was on a boat with a bunch of Communists, but the racist expletives I was taught in advanced infantry training just didn't make any sense in this case. These people were clearly not gooks. They were ordinary, maybe even extraordinary, human beings.

A few miles shy of Go Cong and the open sea we heard the noise of ARVN PT boats. Five of them were coming rapidly upstream towards us. I thought this would surely be the end of my bizarre adventure but as one of the boats pulled alongside, a scrawny ARVN captain asked somewhat reluctantly, "What are you doing with the pineapples?" Muy Ba threw him one and asked him to try it. Our pilot said something about taking them to market. The soldier appeared satisfied and his boat sped away to travel in the safety of the water convoy. I had stayed in my chair with my hat over my eyes. Either I had passed for Vietnamese or the guy just didn't notice or care.

Dinnertime came and to my delight the captain's assistant Tuan prepared rice and fresh fish from Can Duoc. The meal was superb if not exactly French gourmet as I had learned to enjoy in Saigon. I might have preferred homemade ice cream with made from scratch chocolate sauce, but the pineapple was again served sliced and warm.

Once past the many mouths of the Mekong River, Captain Nguyen pointed to a fishing village on the shore and said it was Vinh Chau, his hometown. I noticed a forlorn look on his face and asked if his family was still there. He said," No, we all moved north together right after the events of 1954 made it clear that we would be at war with the Americans."

About an hour later he pointed to shore again and said the lights we could see on our right twinkling in the breeze were in Vinh Loi and that the lights to portside were Con Son Island. The island was home to the notorious prison where National Liberation Front (NLF) soldiers both young and old were kept in tiny tiger cages because they would not renounce their allegiance to the cause of independence. I hadn't yet heard of the prison or the cages but years later remembered the moment when a member of our Congress visited the place and made a big stink about the brutal inhumane conditions. I'm afraid that his efforts may have just encouraged the ARVN forces to kill more POW's.

Captain Nguyen and Tuan took turns at the wheel while the old man, Muy Ba and I enjoyed a leisurely meal with 33 beer, the two-digit name was a gift from the French. The conversation was sparse.

I said, "Why do you think the beer smells of formaldehyde?"

The old man who Muy Ba now called Grandpa Vo, said, "It is just the preservative the French taught us to use since refrigeration was rare in the countryside."

I said, "Well it certainly works." I had tried to drink the cans of beer that came from the states in the miserable hot holds of ships, but they always tasted terrible. "The 33 tastes fresh and natural once you get hooked on the smell. Now I really enjoy it even when it is served warm like this." I caught myself thinking I was especially enjoying it because of the company.

Muy Ba broke my reverie saying, "I prefer pineapple juice." I wasn't sure if she was joking or if Grandpa Vo wouldn't let her drink beer.

"Well," I started, and Vo interrupted me saying, "Of course you are wondering what is happening to you." I agreed with a nod and a tentative yes.

Vo continued, "You have been carefully chosen for a task that is of vital importance for our liberation movement."

I quickly responded. "I want to be unchosen so I can return to my unit and stay out of trouble."

Vo then said, "We will arrive in Singapore in the morning thanks to the speed of this old junk."

"Singapore?" I asked.

Vo answered, "I have to attend a meeting and complete some correspondence. You and Muy Ba can take some time to look around the city. Singapore is an exciting market town. It is too bad the Communist party has been outlawed. We now have to meet our friends clandestinely."

CHAPTER 12

AWOL

I realized that Vo was not just the old man I had seen walking along the street in Ben Luc just yesterday. He may have been old, but he now spoke with strength and vigor which I somehow found reassuring. He didn't leave any room for discussion, so I just wandered off thinking nervously that this unauthorized R & R was turning into quite the escapade. Muy Ba chimed in and said, "How can you decide you don't want to help us if you don't even know what we want you to do."

"Well, now that I've been in Vietnam for nine months, I know the war isn't as simple as I naively thought a year ago. I have learned to love and respect the Vietnamese people and culture. But to help the 'enemy' wouldn't just be illegal for me. It could well mean death for treason if I got caught."

Muy Ba responded, "For now please just let us show you what we think this hideous war is about. Then you can make up your own mind. We will get you back to Ben Luc by Friday. Now let's just walk around the boat." She brushed against me lightly as we started to walk the deck to look for her imaginary zebras. As I held her hand, it became impossible to think rationally about the implications of my conduct.

Evening came and the boat moved swiftly through the calm waters under the smiling moon. Were these not the conditions for the most common and thrilling chemistry experiment ever? As we held hands, we both seemed to realize it felt a lot like love. Later I went to sleep working on a twisted jumble of feelings. The thoughts of her beauty in the pool by the canal and the warmth of her young tender hand offset my concern about being AWOL and I slept peacefully to the rhythm of the big diesel engine.

CHAPTER 13

Singapore

In the morning I awoke with a start. The Luba was silent, and we were barely rocking. I wondered if we were still at sea. I saw that no one was in the hold with me and heard noises above. I brushed my teeth with a washcloth, splashed water on my face and finger combed my scant GI hair. I went up and saw six men unloading the pineapples into a deuce and a half (2 and 1 /2 ton truck). I was relieved to see Muy Ba standing at the rail watching them work and said, "What's going on?"

"Cho ong mon joy." Her good morning sir how are you in Vietnamese with a sweet smile was a fine way to start the day. The more I heard this melodic language the more I liked it. The Vietnamese have perfect pitch. Know the tones or get your eggs in the face instead of over easy!

I was boiling over with questions but just asked, "Where are we and how did we get here?"

"We went through the Straits of Singapore and got to customs at about 5 a.m. There was just a short line and the captain got us through very quickly. You were no problem since you were sleeping soundly. The agent looked at our papers and stamped them with no questions. The pineapples were probably the answer to any questions he might have had."

"Did you give him some pineapple?"

"No way! These guys were trained by the British Colonialists and would have been suspicious had we offered a bribe. There is so much commerce here that it usually goes smoothly. The captain makes two or three trips here a month with no unusual cargo so on visits like this nothing illegal is suspected by the agents."

"Right now, we are at Clifford Pier. Once we finish unloading and get paid for the cargo, we will go under the Benjamin Sheares Bridge and up the Singapore River to dock at the Elgin Bridge near Chinatown where Grandpa Vo will have some meetings."

"And what am I supposed to do?"

"He has asked me to show you around. Singapore is quite an exciting cosmopolitan town. We have nothing like it in Hanoi."

"Sounds good to me," I said.

We left Nguyen and Tuan on the boat and walked along the river on Boat Quay Street. The weather was ideal, and the people were friendly as they nodded or smiled. We soon arrived at destination number one, the Metropole Hotel. Mysteriously reservations had been made and we checked into adjoining rooms with a connecting door.

"Let's take showers."

"What's the use since I have no clean clothes?"

She called me silly again and pushed me towards my room.

"We can go shopping after we clean up."

I took a leisurely bath relishing the simple beauty of clean white porcelain and fluffy cotton towels. The room was utilitarian, clean and fresh. I wondered about paying for the room and the clothes we planned to buy. I didn't have much money and it was all Vietnamese Dong. When Muy Ba knocked, I opened the door. She had changed into the western outfit I had first seen in Ben Luc. She was angelic as she said, "Did you liked it?"

"It's heavenly."

She said, "Let's go!" and away we went. We spent the day seeing the sights that were truly amazing. Singapore was then a newly burgeoning town which had just won independence from the British a few months earlier in 1965. Modern day Singapore dates back to January 29, 1819 when the representative of the British East India Company, Sir Thomas Raffles, stepped ashore. It was then called Singa Pura, meaning Lion City in Sanskrit the ancient language of Hinduism, the classic literary language of India. Most of the population was now Indian, Malay and Chinese. English was still the language that tied the Asians together along with the Europeans in a finely tuned modern city state.

The Europeans seemed to be missing as we walked the streets, but the imprint of the British was visible everywhere in street names like Waterloo, Victoria and Upper Cross. The older buildings were pleasing colonial architecture while the new office towers would have looked at home in Chicago. We shopped just for the bare minimum—underwear, shirt and pants as well as a razor and toothbrush—then stopped for lunch at the astonishing bird singing café. People brought their birds to the restaurant so they could learn to coo and warble new tunes from the other guest birds. It was as if the mixing of human cultures prompted the people to encourage the birds to homogenize as well. The cages were elaborate bamboo castles with lots of swings and toys to keep the musicians happy.

We were happy too as we sat quietly and ate the simple buttered garlic noodles. All around us the locals were enjoying popular local dishes such as roti pratas, pastry stuffed with eggs and onions and nasi biryani which is a saffron rice dish with spicy chicken. We couldn't resist the teh tarik served creamy and hot with a frothy milk topping. I thought about my troubles and good fortune as Muy Ba reveled in the moment. Her comfortable peace with the present contrasted favorably with the hectic pace of high school I had experienced back in Indiana at her age.

Walking back to the hotel we passed the Abdul Gaffoor Mosque, the Burmese Buddhist Temple and the Sri Srinivasa Temple with its monument to the God Vishnu. Muy Ba looked up at the god's many heads and said, "It looks like the sculptor couldn't decide what to make so just threw in everything but the zebra!"

I couldn't argue with that, but I was thinking that the Christians three in one God wasn't that much different. No kidding. Their King James Bible talks about a God known as the Holy Ghost!

Following my vacation-like day—I was thoroughly enjoying my unauthorized R&R—I was relieved to get back to the hotel. We just hung around for a while, then fell asleep arm in arm on the couch in my room. Dinner time rolled around, and we ordered Laksa noodles in curry this time. They came with the same Roti Prata flatbread treat from India that we had liked at lunch. I had a Tiger beer and with no one around to complain we shared it. We then went to our separate rooms for another good night's sleep.

In the morning we wandered back to the boat and sat in the deck chairs waiting for the others to return. We watched the buzz of activity on the pier and the street beyond rickshaws, hawkers pushing their carts full of wares, motor scooters and the odd Rolls Royce competed for space.

They returned all too soon and our pineapple boat captain Nugyen ran immediately to us talking excitedly. Muy Ba then told me, "Grandpa has been called back to Hanoi for an emergency meeting of the Politburo. He must leave immediately, and I have to go with him."

I asked somewhat pathetically, "What about me?"

"You will have to go back to Ben Luc without me this time."

"Do we really need to hurry like this and when can I see you again?"

She said calmly that she would ask Grandpa. They talked for a while as they gathered their things below and I thought he was teasing her but she ran back to me and said cheerfully, "I can probably be back in Ben Luc four weeks from tomorrow. Look for me at the boat or ask about me at the pharmacy." Grandpa grabbed his bag and they headed straight to the first taxi.

CHAPTER 14

Sabre Thrust

The crew and I boarded the boat somewhat dejectedly. Neither Tuan nor Nguyen spoke much English, so we had a speedy and quiet trip back to Vietnam, highlighted by Chinese carryout from a pushcart on Boat Quay Street. Washed down with more Tiger Beer, dinner was so good I thought about writing to General Westmoreland to suggest he switch to Singapore pushcart vendors for our military's dining enjoyment. Troop morale would surely rocket from the good eats. The hammock felt familiar and comfortable. I slept like a healthy happy baby with no worry about my AWOL situation.

After an uneventful return trip from Singapore to Vietnam in the fast and now empty boat, I was miraculously back in Ben Luc Friday morning as Muy Ba had promised I would be when she talked me into heading downriver with her. Once I was dropped off at the pier in the middle of town, the crew turned the boat around and sped downstream. The goodbyes had been cordial, but I gathered the crew did not want to wait around while I might think about running to the base to report them. I walked slowly back to camp with just a quick stop at Ba's stand for a refreshing breakfast of Pho with noodles and beef bones. Ba made it every day with the usual ginger, onions, star anise, cardamom and fresh greens. Back at camp I picked up my gear and looked wistfully at the bunker where I had enjoyed sleeping with the rats. Nobody seemed to pay any attention to me, so I walked through the perimeter where the same big friendly MP was still guarding the gate. I went down the road a few hundred yards to the airfield and waited for a ride back to Cu Chi.

I got back to my desk in the late afternoon and found things winding down for the day at the office. The editor of our newspaper, *The Tropic Lightning News*, stopped at my desk and said, "I'm still short about 200 words for the next issue. Joe said you would probably have something to go with the photos he turned in of the 1st Brigade medics running a clinic in Ben Luc."

I said, "When do you need it?"

"We need to have it on the first chopper to Saigon Monday morning. Anytime you finish this weekend let me know and I'll get it ready to go."

"Fair enough, I'll have something ready by tomorrow afternoon."

I sat down and started to write the story for the paper but could not stop thinking about what I had just been through in the middle of this war. I was sure no one else in the office could even imagine, though Joe probably had an idea. Luckily, I was now alone in the office. My smile went unnoticed as I looked through the window screens that were each 36 by 48 inches and surrounded the bare bones building. It was one of several similar structures here at the headquarters of the division. I was ecstatic! I had gone on my little escapade and no one noticed that I had been gone. This Army was so poorly run, and the Public Information Office so ridiculously overstaffed, that no one cared!

Referring to my notes from another recent trip to the field, I wrote my story:

The 25th Infantry Division Operation "Sabre Thrust" has cleared the main supply route between Saigon and Tay Ninh City. The 70 kilometer stretch of strategically important road had previously been under constant attack by enemy forces in their attempt to stop supply convoys. The operation is being conducted by the 3rd Squadron, 4th Cavalry. The key to their success is mobility; armored personnel carriers, tanks and helicopter gunships.

To date, Sabre Thrust has accounted for 5 VC killed by body count and 14 additional possible kills. Seventy-two Vietnamese who were without proper identification have been detained. Several were found to be draft dodgers while eight were confirmed to be Viet Cong.

And finally, I ended with:
U.S. casualties have been very light.

The article made the front page, so I sent it home to Mom and Dad with this letter:

Hello Mom and Dad,

Stuff outlined in blue is written by me.

Did you see me sleeping under the truck in last week's' paper?

My story about the Cavalry is of course not told too truthfully—but that is my job.

Larry.

CHAPTER 15

The Brothel

Back in Cu Chi on Monday morning, Joe and I got an assignment to go see what was happening at the Michelin plantation near Tay Ninh. We walked down to the helipad and caught a supply chopper heading to the plantation with hot meals for the men of the 2/14 who were now bivouacked there. The stench of those meals did not make us want to eat with the 2/14, so once the chopper landed, we went through security and into the adjacent village for *pommes frites* and Coca Colas. After the tasty lunch we walked a ways then heard some noise. Something was going on up some stairs.

Slowly and quietly, we mounted the stairs. A door was cracked open a bit. I pushed it open all the way without a thought of raising the M-16 that hung at my side. Before us were about thirty Vietnamese women sitting in a circle. Candles were burning and the wonderful smell of incense was in the air. We assumed it was a Buddhist ceremony of some sort and left.

When we got back to the 2/14 base camp we realized we had missed the last chopper back to Cu Chi. So just like that we turned around and went back out through security and started walking to the city. We didn't know if we'd make it or what we'd find but anything seemed better than a night on the cold bare floor of the now abandoned Michelin rubber plantation mansion. We were about two miles out when we heard the putt putt of a 50cc Honda motorcycle. We flagged it down. It was loaded with about 100 loaves of bread and headed for a shop in town. We hopped on. With the little engine straining we were soon on our way in style. At the well-secured bunker on the edge of town our friend was waved through on his putt putt without a second look, but not us. The ARVN troops on duty spoke no English and our Vietnamese was pathetic but after some friendly back and forth with English, Vietnamese and a spattering of French, we were allowed into the city of Tay Ninh.

Curfew was fast approaching in this occupied city, so we were anxious to find a place to sleep. Our pitiful knowledge of the language got us directions to a brothel instead of a cheap hotel. We rang the bell at street level and were welcomed to the entertainment facility on the second floor, just as an MP jeep rolled slowly by looking for curfew breakers like us.

When the first girl was presented topless with flimsy panties, we knew we had made a mistake. We refused her charms and tried in vain to say we just wanted a place to sleep.

The next girl to appear was dressed modestly in a traditional áo dài. Joe said, "Let's show them our money." So, we pulled out our wallets and again said we just wanted a place to sleep and stressed our lack of resources. Our charades failed miserably, and the parade continued.

Next came a modestly dressed older woman. Behind her signaling for me to keep quiet was the lovely Muy Ba who was supposed to be in Hanoi! I was shocked and embarrassed but took the hint and kept my mouth shut. In English she said that Joe could go with the modestly dressed woman who would show him to a bed and leave him in peace. She told me to follow her.

I said to Joe, "Go ahead and get some sleep and I'll be back here in the morning. With Joe looking at me dumbstruck, I took the stairs and followed Muy Ba out the back. Since I had just recently been with her in Singapore and did not expect to see her again for another month, I was happy, shocked and full of questions.

"What are you doing here? Why aren't you in Hanoi? How on earth did you find me here in this brothel? Are you in trouble?" Of course, it was really Muy Ba so she laughed as she pulled me across the street to the USAID office.

The United States Aid To International Development office in Tay Ninh was supposedly part of the U S war effort, but as I soon learned it had pretty much been taken over by the amazing Muy Ba, who held my hand as we entered the office. Linda from Dallas greeted us with a fine southern smile and asked Muy Ba who her new friend was. That made me wonder how many other G.I.'s she had taken here to further her cause.

Linda said, "I'll bet you're here to accept the latest rice shipment." Muy Ba said, "Oh, I'm not worried but yes I would like to count the bags." We walked into the adjacent warehouse and there it was: an impressive pile of one thousand 20-pound bags clearly labeled Basmati Rice Texas USA.

Muy Ba signed for the shipment, thanked Linda and said, "Tan Tan will be here in the morning with the truck and your cash."

Then we walked, back towards the center of town, our hands brushing each other, and used the side entrance to the bakery, where her brother Tan Tan greeted us.

At last, the explanations began. She had been in Hanoi for a while but had to come back south early because her little brother was worried about a security breach at the bread factory his squad ran. It was just two miles toward Cambodia from the plantation where the 2/14 Wolfhounds were dug in. "How could he possibly have known that he was picking up Joe and me out on the highway?"

"He didn't know it was you, silly," she said. I don't know why but I still was thrilled to hear her call me silly. Then she said, "You sure looked cute when you barged in on our Young Communist Girls Brigade meeting."

"What?"

"You were upstairs in the village by the Michelin Plantation when Joe and I opened the door?" She explained that the Viet Cong were strong in the area and said that I shouldn't be surprised. Tan Tan had stopped to see her and drop off some bread on the way to town and she had told him about seeing us. So naturally when he saw two crazy Americans walking alone, he thought it would be us and cheerfully took us along.

"OK things are starting to add up," I said. "But what made you think we would be visiting the brothel?"

Muy Ba looked a little sad, but then said, "I felt bad when I saw you go there, but then I listened and peeked through the curtain. Once I discovered you were just looking for a hotel room, I made my plan to kidnap you again and here we are!"

"The communist princess of kidnappers strikes again! Now that you have saved me, what do you plan to do with me?"

We talked about taking a walk or going to a restaurant and then she said, "Do you know about the Cao Dai religion?"

I said I had never heard of it. She was shocked by my "ignorant."

"You mean ignorance."

Then looking concerned she said, "That doesn't sound very nice."

I soon learned that Cao Dai is the third largest religion in Vietnam. Nearly 90 percent of the people are Buddhist and about 10 percent are Christians. The Cao Dai are too small a group to even be statistically counted—just a few hundred thousand. Most of them live in the south.

Joe and I dutifully went to the temple in the morning and were rewarded with an enthusiastic welcome by a crowd of children in the expansive courtyard near the massive front doors. The kids were amazed by the hair on my arms and showed it by petting me like an exotic zoo animal.

Knowing nothing about this religion—our troops were after all there to kill not to know—we were surprised to see the massive picture of Victor Hugo, the author of *Les Miserables*, on the front wall along with Buddha and Sun Yat Sen, the Chinese revolutionary of 1911. These were apparently the religion's three saints.

After the educational tour of the temple, Muy Ba, Joe and I had a leisurely lunch of pho and rice and talked about the Cao Dai.

[After the war, Cao Dai communities could be found all over the world, including several in California. Total membership would exceed 5 million.]

I could see that Muy Ba had great respect for Cao Dai and asked her, "How can you as a Communist and an atheist like the Cao Dai?"

"The Cao Dai teach love and brotherhood and promote harmony between all races. To honor the best of all religions has been the goal of Cao Dai since its founding in 1926 in Vietnam. All of the Viet Cong leadership in Tay Ninh Province is Cao Dai and there has never been a conflict with the goals of the religion and the nationalist independence goals of our party."

And then as if on cue, Joe said "Go ahead and talk religion all you want, but I want to get back to base and catch a chopper to Cu Chi."

I said, "How do you propose to get back?"

He said, "We can hitchhike again."

Muy Ba said, "Wait until Tan Tan finishes dealing with the rice shipment and he will give you a ride back." She then put another smile on my face saying, "I will be in Ben Luc as scheduled and *hoping* we can meet there again."

"Before we go," I said, "I want to ask you about a sign we found out in the boonies near the rubber plantation. It was written in English suggesting that the Americans leave.

"We put up lots of signs. What did it say?"

I showed her the photo I had taken of a handsome, young, American soldier smiling as he posed for me next to the sign which read:

U.S. officers and men

The Vietnamese people are not enemies of the American people. If anyone invaded your country, massacred your compatriots, destroyed your homes, villages and property, how would you react to all that?

Oppose the U.S. aggressive war in S.V.N.

Peace for Vietnam!

"Clearly I didn't write it, "she said. "I would have started Officers and mens! No matter how hard I try to get Tan Tan and his friends to use better words on their signs, they still make silly mistakes like that."

That was all the confirmation I needed. Tan Tan and his friends had done it and seemed to be better at English than Muy Ba. Tan Tan just smiled and revved his engine, so Joe and I hopped on the little red motorcycle. Without the load of bread, the ride was fast and smooth. We got to the chopper as it was about to take off and were soon flying over the impressive Cao Dai temple in military style with an M60 machine gun for company. Cao Dai literally meant high tower and from the air at about 500 feet I could almost reach out and touch it. The pilot noticed our interest and asked if we would like a closer look. The thought of him diving down and scaring those lovely children prompted an urgent "No" from me and we continued back Cu Chi without incident. A few months earlier I had gone on a booze run from Cu Chi to Saigon with a couple of totally mindless hot-dogging pilots who were on a mission to get me to vomit. They had flown straight at trees then pulled up and seemed to bounce over the trees at the last second. When they saw a woman and her child walking on a dike, they dove straight at them and again pulling up just in time to miss them but surely inflicting trauma that would never end. I can't say I was sorry to hear it, but just a few weeks later the two crashed their $5 million gunship and died.

On that trip I took advantage of the visit to the PX and bought a lovely bottle of Mateus Rose. Not that we planned to celebrate their demise a few days later but when we attempted to force the cork into the bottle, it broke. Our non-celebration was all over my desk and our jungle fatigues. The gods of the killer choppers got us!

CHAPTER 16

Bombs away

My next assignment was to walk along the outside perimeter of the 25th INF Division base at Cu Chi with some support staff that wanted to experience the war outside the concertina wire that surrounded the base. The base provided housing and offices for 12,000 soldiers as well as some Red Cross donut dollies who gawked as we peed into six inch round tubes sticking out of the ground at a comfortable angle.

In January 1967, John J. McCormick took over command of the 3rd Squadron, 4th Cavalry. He had spent the first six months of his tour behind a desk and transferred to the 25th Infantry Division probably to get some combat duty which would give him a better chance for advancement in the military. His new unit was also primarily a support unit. He soon discovered the company was full of others itching for action. So, they formed the McCormick's Raiders made up of cooks, mechanics and typists. After some special training the motley crew was given the assignment to scour the outside of the perimeter looking for booby traps. I was sent along from the Public Information Office to document the adventure.

After a couple of uneventful hours, the Raiders got bored and lazy. I was shocked to see the lead vehicle driving toward an obvious anti-tank mine. For a moment I considered crouching to get a good photograph of the coming carnage which I could show Muy Ba, who would be so proud of the successful effort by the local explosives brigade. I had already switched sides in the war but yelled as loud as I could for the volunteers to stop. They looked at me with my black PIO armband and thought I was crazy for taking charge. The Captain got off his perch on the lead tank and walked my way asking what all the yelling was about. I pointed out a bamboo stick that I thought was the trigger for an antitank mine. The green captain told everyone to get back then pulled the pin on a grenade, placed it at the mine and ran for cover.

It was an antitank mine all right. The secondary explosion shook the whole neighborhood and would surely have killed everyone in the APC and would have killed or wounded many more walking nearby. I was happy that I had saved the Americans and sad that I had betrayed the Vietnamese. I went back to the office and wrote my story about the volunteers without a mention of the antitank mine and my quandary. Forty-six years later I am still torn by the moral dilemma caused by the incident. It is comforting to think that if I had opted to take the photo instead of yelling, I would likely have been killed.

There were other times when I had to save the newly arrived Americans. I remember walking with a patrol by a house in Tay Ninh. The guy in front of me reached to open a gate and I yelled at him to stop. Because I was experienced, I immediately saw that it was booby trapped with a hand grenade.

Payday was coming up and most guys were short so poker was played in the office for payday stakes. A sergeant E6 was our old timer. He sucked on a messy cigar that was not lit the whole time he played. He played poker really well and claimed to have sent lockers full of money home during his previous tours.

They called me raise a quarter Larry and that's just what I did. Hour after hour flew by with greenbacks, Vietnamese Dong and IOU's flying in and out of the kitty. On the biggest pot of the night I bet the farm on an ace high straight and lost to a straight flush. I paid with an IOU!

I was out in the field working when payday came, and the holder of the IOU probably gave up on me since I had transferred down to the 1st Brigade to start my chaplain's assistant gig. I eventually showed up and paid to his delight.

It was at one of these games that I heard the old timer on his third tour in Vietnam tell about the headquarters brigade being attacked by mortars where he was stationed up north. We thought it could never happen to us but of course it soon did.

I didn't by any means suffer my misgivings about my place in the war in isolation. I wrote to my old Wheaton College friend Wally Matthews about my growing disenchantment with the war. I talked with my coworkers, especially Joe. I talked to the new Major and convinced him we were on the wrong side in the war, and I finally talked to my parents. On March 11, 1967 I wrote to them:

...I'll just be here inside the base camp at Cu Chi or in Saigon on vacation or out of the country on vacation between now and when I get home this summer. I hope that makes you people feel a bit better. It certainly relaxes me now that I think about it. I have seen all the war that I could ever want to see. I talk to Wally a lot about my feeling toward the US's intervention here but haven't said much to you about it perhaps because I thought you would feel better about my being here not knowing how I feel but now I have decided to talk a bit about it.

I'm on the side of the so called Vietniks, the Quakers and Bobby Kennedy. And very, very strongly so. Johnson's liberality with money is hard enough to take, but his liberality with lives is totally impossible to take. There are over a thousand people a week being killed here and it is all in vain. The only people fighting here for a cause are the Viet Cong and North Vietnamese. If we would get out, they could soon have control of the country and the fighting would be over. And the government the people of Vietnam would then have would be a lot better for them than the one the Americans are attempting to establish. So that is a bit about how I feel. I could not dislike anyone more than I dislike Johnson. I hope that because I am here you don't feel obligated to support the administration and Johnson in this ridiculous war.

Well now you know how I feel. If you disagree with me quite strongly as I think you might, please ask me questions about it, don't just get mad about it and Dad

I would certainly like at least a long week-end at the Abinadawn River when I get home so please think about arranging it. How is your Mercedes?
  Lots of love, Larry

Writing the letter home sure got me thinking about the family's wonderful camping trips to Canada. In 1948 my family made its first trek to the Aubinadong River in Ontario Canada north of Sioux Sault Marie. We traveled in a 1940 Willys that Dad bought for $50 and worked on for a month to get it ready for the trip. An Indian who ran the general store at Aubrey Falls on the river told us where we could find an abandoned logger's cabin on the river. We eventually had several wonderful vacations there, the last one with the family in 1958.

We took my high school friend Mac along that time. While Mom and Dad were sweeping out the cabin and moving in our boxes of supplies, Mac and I hopped in the big blue fiberglass canoe, revved the engine and zoomed upstream to a prime fishing spot. On my first excited cast into the swirling river, I tipped the canoe and dumped all our fishing gear as well as the outboard motor that had been hastily attached to the flat back of the one-ton fiberglass canoe from Sears. When we finally got back to the cottage Mom was mad, sad, crying and in a funny way happy to see us back alive.

Dad went back to the scene of the loss with us and piece by piece our gear emerged from the bottom on the hook that Dad had made from a coat hanger. He hooked the motor too, but it wouldn't budge so I followed the line down and moved it up hill a bit towards shore. I came up for air then went down again and managed to get it near the surface where Dad and Mac grabbed it.

Writing now in 2013 I see I should tell you who Wally was. We were on the wrestling team together at Wheaton College along with Speaker of the United States House of Representatives, Dennis Hastert, if you can imagine that. We shared an apartment for a while at 809 North Wabash Street while I worked for the Cook County Department of Public Aid and he went to Northwestern University Law School and studied Russian literature at The University of Chicago simultaneously!

He wrote to me regularly and tried to turn me against the war.

I think I changed for the most part because of what I saw in the actual war but the material he sent no doubt helped as well. In particular I remember the Playboy magazine from Wally with the Muhammad Ali interview. I recall that Ali said as a reason to refuse to go to the war "I ain't got nothing against no Viet Cong, they never called me nigger or made me sit at the back of the bus" Ali lost his Heavyweight Boxing Champion of the World title for refusing to go to the war. He also gave up millions and millions of dollars in earnings by not going. I, on the other hand, read Steven Crane's *Red Badge of Courage* as a kid and watched the John Wayne movie *The Ballad of the Green Berets* when I was 25 years old and then did the easy thing. I fell for the hoopla, joined the Army, and went to war. I simply floated downstream with the crowd while the men and women of conscience somehow found a way to not go. I cannot over-emphasize my respect for those courageous young men who went to Canada to avoid the war.

A few days later I asked if another story was needed on the troops down in Ben Luc. It was one thing to tell Mother I would stay safe on the base but quite another to stay away from Muy Ba so off I went to Ben Luc hoping to find her. I wandered down to the airfield planning to take the first ride I could get to either Ben Luc or Saigon. Saigon it was.

I resisted the temptation to go back to the Saigon Health Club for another "No Sex" massage and went straight to the bus station. The next bus to Ben Luc didn't leave for three hours so I caught a pedicab and asked to go to the Continental Hotel. The cabby's muscular legs and fast clip reminded me of the young man who had chased Joe and I away from his wife who was working in her vegetable garden. When I paid him triple the fare, I thought about what Viet Cong unit he might be in. It would still be another year but when the Tet offensive started in 1968, he and his comrades emerged and attacked government facilities all over town.

The following is from *Victory in Vietnam* first published in Hanoi in 1988 and later published in English by the University of Kansas Press:

In Saigon-Gia Dinh, during the days before Tet the sapper teams assigned to attack the primary targets within the city dispersed into cells, and traveling by many different routes, joined the flood of people in the streets doing their Tet shopping, secretly hiding their troops and delivering additional explosives and weapons to cache in the homes of our agents.

During the night of 30-31 January 1968, the sound of our guns attacking Saigon rang out simultaneously at the U.S. Embassy, Independence Palace, the Puppet General Staff headquarters, the Puppet Navy Headquarters, Tan Son Nhat Airbase and many other locations. (Victory in Vietnam pp. 219, 220)

The Tet offensive was a great victory for the Vietnamese, and they knew it but the American leadership assumed that since the Vietnamese forces retreated from Hue, the ancient capital of Vietnam, after occupying it for a month they had been defeated. They realized much later that the images of NLF flags flying over our embassy and of our puppet allies being routed wherever they engaged with the highly motivated Communists had dealt a fatal blow to support for the war by ordinary Americans.

Muy Ba's enthusiasm for the overall success of the coordinated attacks all over the South was tempered by the loss of eight of her heroic sappers, guerilla soldiers, from the 3rd Commando unit that had attacked the Independence Palace. Explosives were used to demolish the main gate to the Palace which was the home of the American-backed president. The two cells of fighters that followed through the gate were forced to battle two battalions of ARVN soldiers on Nguyen Do Street.

CHAPTER 17

Rest and Relaxation

When my one-year tour in Vietnam was up, I still had six months left in the Army. The Army had a policy to let soldiers extend their tours and then get out of the Army early. To avoid six months of boring duty back in the states I extended my tour in Vietnam for three months. Despite my promise to Mom to stay away from combat and my regular attempts to go on R&R, I did manage two more wonderful vacations in those three months.

The first was to Taiwan. I fell for the Pan Am flight attendant on the trip and spent all my time there sightseeing, eating and loving with her. What an exotic beauty she was. Her father was a Swedish diplomat stationed in Haiti and her mother was a coal black Haitian. I could not get enough of her caramel skin. She seemed to know how to make the best of the situation as well. Midway through our first erotic explorations she said, "Massage my clitoris. I cheerfully complied with my hand and was quickly told, "No, use your tongue."

I slowly tongued my way to the target. We had the lights on multiplying the sensations from cool sheets to beautiful, soft wonderful skin. I wondered if Ulla's fine warm, brown, body is what Mother was trying to protect me from when she sent the Playboy calendar full of white girls. Apparently, I passed Ulla's sophistication test. We finally slept comfortably arm and leg together.

We had breakfast in the lobby where Ulla seemed proud to show off her whisker burns to the rest of her crew as they wandered in. After eating we hopped a cab for the quick trip to Yangmingshan National Park, the smallest national park on the island of Taiwan, where we toured as if on cloud nine. Yangmingshan is famous for its hot springs and geothermal thrillers. We borrowed suits and cheerfully cooked away for an hour with the other tourists.

This holiday ended way too soon so we made plans to meet again as soon as possible in Bangkok. Somehow, we managed to coordinate trips to Bangkok a few weeks later. My short flight from Saigon arrived several hours before hers so I had a walk around the neighborhood. Many businesses advertised in English. They offered Thai food, massage, jewelry or jewelry, massage. Massage seemed to be the theme of the neighborhood right by the fancy hotel. Instead of offering massage no sex as at the Saigon Health Club, these places offered "Two Girls Your Choice."

With love on my mind I checked into the Hotel Intercontinental alone and went to the lobby to wait for Ulla to arrive. Her crew got there right on time but sadly without Ulla.

Her friends told me that she had been arrested in Taiwan by immigration. She had attempted to pass through customs with the rest of the crew but because she was not a U.S. citizen she was busted and sent back to the states by Pan Am where she continued working out of Miami for Eastern Airlines. I had sent her roses. What a waste!

I went out to the pool broken hearted and thinking about what to do next. I started talking with the only other bather in the pool. She was from Kansas City, Missouri, and was waiting for her husband who was a U.S. Army general of some sort. He was supposed to be on my Pan Am flight from Saigon but apparently had missed it. As we bounced around in the water, we noticed a beautiful young woman dancing nude with herself in a room on the second floor and very close to the pool. She seemed to think her tinted windows kept our eyes out along with the sun. But there she was dancing away with a lovely pointed breast in each hand.

Soon my swim mate was encouraging me to water dance with her. She bounced up close to me then wrapped her long luscious legs around my leg and erotically swam backwards with her foot pulling at my happy Johnson as I admired the tits dancing in the second story window and fantasized that I was with Ulla and these two together. I eventually realized that she wanted to take off my trunks and party so back to her nearby room we went. She was no Ulla but her desperate caresses eventually seemed to satisfy us both and I was well on my way to getting over my ruined plans. I suggested dinner but she had to stay by the phone and hope that the general made the next flight.

Back on the street again I decided to see what girl girl massage was all about. I walked up to the second-

CHAPTER 18

Air America

Back at the luxury hotel, I enjoyed a long leisurely bath and then checked out for my evening flight back to Saigon.

The flight was delayed so when we got to Tan Son Nhut Airport, our ride to Cu Chi had already left and an E6 sergeant was herding the group to a transit tent for a captive night. When I realized what the plan was, I decided to enhance my holiday with a taxi ride to the Tan Loc Hotel. It looked like the same old blue and yellow cab that Tim and I had taken to Saigon from the airport several months ago. It also took me through Cholon, the Chinese district before dropping me in front of the Tan Loc.

I didn't get the usual friendly greeting from the owner and soon found out why. She would not release my suitcase full of civilian clothes and personal items or check me in until I paid an overdue bill. You probably remember Timmy puff puffing on his cigar when Ed Bishop and I picked him up on one of our clandestine trips to Saigon. A month or so ago he had taken a gang from the 2/14 Wolfhounds to the Tan Loc to show off the place. Unfortunately, I was part of the party. We all trudged up the front stairs to the restaurant on the top floor. It was not the gem that was the Continental Hotel but along with its' low ceilings, open windows and slowing circulating fans, it had girls, girls and more girls. They were numbered and my favorite was Muy Chin, number 19. She was Chinese and had children who stayed in Cholon with grandma. She rode the bus to work at the "restaurant."

The medic for the squad was a big guy, six-two easily and 220 pounds. He was also the banker. I watched a bit amazed as he peeled off bills to pay for the girls and noted in a ledger the guy's remaining balance. Before the money changed hands, a condom had to be shown with a promise to use it. Sex ed at the Tan Loc. We all enjoyed delicious steaks with incredible fresh picked wild mushrooms swimming in a dark onion butter sauce. Someone here may well have learned to cook at Le Cordon Bleu Paris. Coming from a meat and potatoes family in Indiana, I was regularly amazed at the breadth of French culinary excellence retained at so many restaurants here in what Graham Greene famously called the Paris of the Orient.

The medic banker I soon learned didn't gain the trust of the troops by paying restaurant tabs. At the count of three we all got up and headed for the rear stairs. Down on the street the others laughed and hooted about the free dinner and the fine girls.

Then I just worried about facing the music which was now. I ended up paying the entire bill for the Wolfhounds dinner and then went meekly to my room with a lot less cash.

I phoned my friend Marco who flew for Air America. As a CIA pilot he had a lot of free time between assignments, so he ran some businesses in Saigon. I went on the rounds with him one evening and was so shocked by his audacity that I didn't think to congratulate or condemn. He ran nightclubs that served women and girls and drinks. While I sat by the entrance entranced by the action at our first stop, he went to two cash registers and collected bundles of cash while leaving some paperwork. The same scene was repeated at two other clubs.

Even though he had all those good-time girls working for him, he wanted to get to know the German women on the hospital ship, so I arranged a double date for us. Once was enough for these good Germans. Marco's long slicked back hair and "Women are shit" frat boy look was more than Suzie and Delores could handle, so that was our one and only double date.

The next time I was back in town I arranged to go out with Delores Mussa from the ship. Suzie had gone back to Germany and had been replaced by Delores in more ways than planned. I had been fantasizing about her lovely blond hair for some time and now proceeded to bring the fantasy to life. I picked up a tin of liver sausage at the PX on the way to the ship. She was waiting at the gangplank and we went straight to my room at the Tan Loc.

As we worked on our language lessons, I slowly undressed her one kiss at a time. I lingered first at one lovely breast and then the other. I gently nibbled my way past her pulsating belly button then opened the liver sausage and gave her a taste. I spread some on her legs near the fine blond hair I was craving. As I ate my way towards the delicious target that Langston Hughes referred to as the Gates of Heaven, she stretched her arms over her head and lifted her knees while guiding my face. Yes, when I entered her, I knew I was in heaven.

We then went for dinner at Le Steak de Saigon. The *steak frites* was a fine choice then and probably now as well. It was at some French colonial style restaurant that I learned how good ice cream could be. It came after the meal automatically. It was made in house as was the chocolate sauce. My mouth still waters at the thought. All it takes is baking chocolate, fresh unsalted butter, vanilla and some pure cane sugar. I don't suppose Julia Child learned her trade here but the sauce Béarnaise was exactly the same as Muy Ba was preparing for me a few years later in Chicago with Julia's M*astering The Art of French Cooking* turned to page 83. The wonderful old recipe called for wine vinegar, dry white wine, minced shallots or green onions, fresh tarragon, salt and pepper, egg yolks and fresh unsalted butter.

Once we got back to the ship, Ms blonde Mussa realized she had forgotten her umbrella so back we went in a panic. I don't know who had given it to her, but she sure was relieved once it was retrieved. Another time after returning her to the ship I realized I had left or lost my wallet at the restaurant so back I hurried. The new diners sitting in our booth let me check behind them and there it was still stuffed with several hundred hard-earned black-market dollars.

Back at the Tan Loc I was not yet ready to call it a day, so I went up to the restaurant to say hello to Muy Chin, my regular good time girl from the club upstairs, and have a beer. She asked if she could stop by my room after work and I said "Sure." I just had one small twin bed, but we slept well together after a bit of loverly hugging. Muy Chin and I shared a cab in the morning. We had coffee on the street near her home in Cholon then I went alone to the airport where I caught an early flight back "home" to Cu Chi.

I had told some friends about my plans to meet Ulla in Bangkok so now I had to tell them the plans fell through. They offered sympathy and I put my name on the list for whatever R&R happened to come up next with an empty seat.

The office was quiet. The new editor, corporal Ricky Hollister from northern California, was busy as usual perfecting someone else's story. When he stuck his pencil behind his ear at the usual cocky angle, I started to write.

May13th, 1967
Dear Mom and Dad,
Well, my vacation is over and I am back to work. Like you said I would probably be in the letter I got from you last night. I got back to Saigon on the 9th and to Cu Chi on the 11th. I thought I would probably have some mail so I did not mind coming back and sure enough I had a lot of mail. From you and Wally and the Ellch's. Got the box of cookies with bouillon cubes too. Thanks, they were quite good. Next time stuff like potato chips or strings and beef jerky (and I mean jerky) and cracker jacks would be quite nice.
Formosa is a beautiful place and I had perhaps the best vacation I'll have in a good while. Yes, the girl was that good. Her name is Ulla. She is a hostess for Pan American Airlines and she is just so sweet and pretty that I could not help but like her. How fortunate I was. She flies R&R flights regularly. She is based in Hong

Kong. Well, I was on her flight to Formosa and we got along well enough that she agreed to a date for that evening. And then we really did get along and I discovered that she would be in Formosa for the entire week of my vacation. She had two trips to Saigon but came back both evenings. So we had three days and five nights. Pretty good. We went to the beach, riding in the mountains and visited some beautiful parks and museums.

So my spirits are up again.

Funniest problem I have for Vietnam. Three girls. Two from the same part of Germany. Olga is writing such good letters that I have decided to quit writing her for a while. She scares me a bit. Carol in Saigon was so friendly when I got back to Saigon from Taipei that I have decided I had better stay away from her for a while. And Ulla is now based in Miami so I can't see her and she is the one I really want to see! So with three girls, I actually have none right now. So I work. Ha Ha.

Glad to hear all is well at home.

Perhaps by the time you get this you will even be having a bit of good weather. I hope so. The weather here is very enjoyable now. The monsoon is back. So it is not so dry. Yesterday we had a big wind. I am living at First Brigade again and here about five buildings out of 15 that we live in were blown to the ground. Roofs went flying away. Quite exciting. Mine did not blow down so I didn't mind so much. Yes I'm bad.

You can still use my old address. I'm not in the company at First Brigade like I was before. I just live here. It is really a good change. For the last couple of weeks at the other place before I went on holiday they were getting us up at 5:30. Ouch. Now I can sleep till

8 if I care to. I won't be home until July, about the 28th
but that is soon enough.
    Expo 67 sounds fine--I certainly hope to get to it.
    Glad to hear you two are too and perhaps we can
go together.
    Love Larry

With my work done for the day I wandered back to my hooch, picked up a *Newsweek* article Wally had sent and read myself back to sleep. I awoke with a start and decided to go back to Ben Luc and look for Muy Ba. With notebook in hand I went back to the office and asked Ricky if he had something special for me to do. Unfortunately, he did so my plans for Ben Luc were put on hold. A request had come down for the paper to run some stories showing how well our military was meshing with the ARVN in the battle to win the hearts and minds of the people.

CHAPTER 19

Operation Phoenix

I was pleasantly surprised when the next issue of *Tropic Lightning News* came out. Page 5 opened with this:

PFC Larry Ryan of the 25th Division's Admin Company was awarded first prize and $25 in the division's Combat Photography Contest sponsored by Division special Services. PFC Ryan won the first-place prize of $25 for his 3"x5" color slide of a 3rd Sqdn, 4th Cav, tank securing Highway 1.

The photo was also featured on the inside back cover of the *Tropic Lightning Ambush*, a photo-filled, slick magazine that the office put out once a quarter. (When I read the entire magazine many years later, I found myself charmed by the simplicity of the friendly VC story and saddened by a Joe Kramer cartoon since he was killed soon after.)

With just a few days left before my flight back to San Francisco, I hung around the PIO Cu Chi office and pretended to work as I dreamed of the future. The weather was perfect in Cu Chi as usual, so I took leisurely walks around the perimeter of the base. Learning to slow down was a trick I mastered early on to avoid sweaty discomfort. As long as I drank enough water, the Army issued jungle fatigues were incredibly comfortable. The jungle boots worn with first rate wool socks were the best footwear I ever owned. (Because I was through with the Army, I left all that military issue material behind, but as soon as I got back to San Francisco and saw how popular military clothing was in the antiwar counterculture, I knew I had made a mistake.)

Muy Ba and Tan Tan were both back in Hanoi so I didn't need to think about making excuses for another trip down to Ben Luc. She and her father, Vo Nguyen Giap, were having an animated discussion about the progress of the war against the Americans in the south. Muy Ba said "They call it Operation Phoenix." Mark Zepezauer in his book *The CIA'S Greatest Hits* describes the operation:

Following the deaths of JFK and Ngo Dinh Diem, it was only a matter of time before U.S. combat troops became involved in Vietnam. Within days of the JFK assassination in November 1963, President Johnson had reversed JFK's plan to withdraw U.S. personnel by the end of 1965. As LBJ told one impatient general, "Just get me elected; you can have your damn war."

In August 1964, the CIA and related military intelligence agencies helped fabricate a phony

Vietnamese attack in the Gulf of Tonkin off North Vietnam. This supposed act of North Vietnamese aggression was used as the basis for escalating US involvement.

In March 1965, US troops began pouring into Vietnam. Nine years of backing the French, another nine years of backing Diem and two more years of CIA operations had failed. From this point on, the US Army took over the war effort.

Since the Vietnamese people over-whelmingly supported their own National Liberation Front (the NLF, or "Viet Cong" as we called it), the Army began destroying villages, herding people into internment camps, weeding out the leaders and turning the countryside into a "free-fire zone" (in other words, shoot anything that moves).

The CIA still had a role to play, however. Called Operation Phoenix, it was an assassination program plain and simple. The idea was to cripple the NLF by killing influential people like mayors, teachers, doctors, tax collectors-anyone who aided the functioning of the NLF's parallel government in the South.

Many of the "suspects" were tortured and some were tossed from helicopters during interrogation. William Colby, the CIA official in charge of Phoenix (he later became director of the CIA), insisted this was all part of "military necessity," though he admitted to Congress that he really had no idea how many of the 20,000 killed were Viet Cong and how many were "loyal" Vietnamese.

Colby's confusion was understandable, since Phoenix was a joint operation between the US and the South Vietnamese, who used it as a means of extortion, a protection racket and a way to settle *vendettas. Significantly, the South Vietnamese estimated the Operation Phoenix death toll at closer to 40,000. Whatever the exact number, there's no question the killings were necessary---after all, we were trying to prevent a blood bath.*

I was saddened when Muy Ba told me about talking to her father while trying to hold back her tears. "My good friend Vien was taken up in a helicopter by the Americans who were not wearing uniforms. Two others from his sapper squad were taken with him. While we watched the helicopter rise above the village and circle erratically Vien came tumbling down. We ran to him, but he was already dead when we got to him. A few days later his friends told us that he had refused to answer the agents' questions, so they pushed him out. At his funeral his mother cried uncontrollably while his two younger brothers vowed to take his place and help Uncle Ho rid the country of the Americans."

She told me that her father said nothing as he held her close then took her hand and walked with her to the park by the lake across the street from their house. Finally he asked her about me.

She said she told him that I would be going home to Chicago soon and wanted her to join me and help in the American antiwar effort.

She told me he then said, "I know Larry is an honorable person who has truly learned to love our people but if you go your mother may never see you again and she will be very sad."

"Can't you take her to Singapore or Paris where we could meet?"

"I know you love him very much and I trust you to do what's best for everyone. I have been talking to our attorney, John Le Chan, in Chicago about your Larry Ryan. He is familiar with the immigration requirements for Vietnamese women who want to join their husbands in the states. He assures me that as a girlfriend you have no chance of going legally."

"So, what can I do?" she sobbed.

"Le Chan tells me that the sooner you get married the better."

"Where would I get married and would mother ever forgive me?"

"I have talked to your mother about it already and she is now busy making plans. The wedding will be as soon as you and Larry agree to meet in Ben Luc. Larry needs to work fast on legal documents since he will be going back to Chicago in July."

"What kind of documents?"

"He needs to write to his parents and friends and tell them about his plans. He needs to apply through the military to take you back with him. I'm told that the letters and the formal application through the military are the kinds of evidence that will make it easy for you to go.

"This all seems so sudden to me. What about the war? Do you think it is the right thing to do?"

"You can talk to your mother about it and then decide in the morning."

After telling me about this incredibly exciting conversation with her father, she went on to tell me that her mother was excited and looking forward to the trip to Ben Luc. Every time the family had gone south in the past because of the war she had been left behind to worry. This time she would be going along and Muy Ba said she was very happy.

Muy Ba told me that she stayed awake most of the night but finally slept deeply in the early morning. When her mom cheerfully called her to breakfast, she told me she had been dreaming about her first trip down the river with me. The dream left her with a warm feeling and a smile. Her mother asked if she had slept well but could tell with a quick glance that she was fine.

Muy Ba told me that her mother told her they would fly to Singapore then go across the South China Sea with wonderful crew she had heard so much about.

Mother said "We will fly into Singapore and then go across to the river in the pineapple boat. I have heard so much about the boat and the wonderful crew that I can't wait to see it. And to think that I have you and Larry and the war to thank for the opportunity! Dad suggested we shop for a dress for you in Singapore, but I said I want you to get married in the same dress my mother wore for her wedding. Look, I brought it out for you to try on. I think you are exactly the size she was."

"Please help me put it on. Oh yes it fits just right. I love the red. The color lasted all these years."

"Oh, it hasn't been that long! And now for the ao dai which is so elegant. The yellow border looks just like new. It has been well protected in the back closet. I once felt bad that I had not let you play with it but now look at you! I'm so happy I could cry!"

"Oh mom!"

"I will talk to our friend at the pharmacy in Ben Luc and have him save a date for us. To be sure he will have time to prepare a proper feast, we need to let him know the date right away.

"Oh mom! What if Larry changes his mind?"

Muy Ba got word to Larry that they needed to meet soon in Ben Luc. She said she would be waiting for him and he needed to bring his friend Joe along.

In Cu Chi Larry got the message from his friend Tuan the 1st Brigade interpreter. He asked Tuan when he was supposed to be in Ben Luc but all Tuan could say was, "It sounds very important so you must go now."

CHAPTER 20

Back to Ben Luc

While walking around Ben Luc after the wedding Muy Ba told Larry what it had been like getting the wedding party together in Hanoi.

"Dad and our whole family, without Tan Tan, who was busy running the bakery in Tay Ninh, piled into the taxi at their front door. It was early and mist was rising from Hoan Kiem Lake across the street. Only the very top of Turtle Tower in the center of the lake was visible. Hanoi was about to come to life but now the peace and quiet of this beautiful city of lakes were real.

"Mother had packed her best gown which she had worn to many state banquets. She fondly remembered being complimented by a young handsome Fidel Castro as Ho Chi Minh smiled at her.

"The Soviet ambassador was at all the functions as required but never noticed her dress or smiled at her. It was as if he didn't even see her. Catering to the general's wife was clearly not his assignment. He may well have been planning the next phase of the training for the heroic anti-aircraft brigades on some of those occasions.

"The flight on Singapore Air was smooth and speedy. A taxi took us immediately to Boat Quay Street where the pineapple boat was waiting. Captain Nguyen (sounds like win), alerted to Madame's curiosity about the pushcart cuisine available here, had the Chinese chicken already in the hold for the trip. He also had plenty of Tiger Beer in the cooler.

"They cleared customs and were on their merry way across the South China Sea before noon. The deep black crystal-clear waters were rhythmically churned into a four-foot-high V shaped wake by the powerful, perfectly tuned diesel engine. The pleasant humming of the Luba soon put the wedding party to sleep.

"Father awoke well into the trip and cheerfully woke Mother with the offer of a bottle of beer. She cheerfully accepted. Once everyone had a beer, Captain Nguyen offered a toast to me and my American Larry Ryan. We all loved the dinner from the pushcart on Boat Quay Street but Mom was just plain ecstatic.

"On our trip up the Mekong to Ben Luc, Tuan pointed out the hidden channel they had often used to go up to the village where Larry befriended the dog and practiced his language skills at the small café. I thought about my leisurely bath in the clear sandy pool and wondered if Larry Ryan had picked up the binoculars to watch me as I had hoped. I had practiced the pose that reminded Larry of Marilyn Monroe. My mother had taught me well in the best Buddhist tradition."

Joe and I were about to head for the landing strip when on a whim I asked my good friend and boss Major

Fleece who had recently arrived from Northern Virginia to come along and have a look at Ben Luc. The Major said, "I have nothing better to do and have been wondering why you and Joe spend so much time there, so why not. When are we leaving?"

I answered, "Now! Joe and I will go down to the heliport and hold the chow chopper until you get there, so please hurry."

When the chopper finally lifted off, I felt the usual thrill as the base receded below and the picture-perfect rice paddies appeared in the distance. When a neat row of B52 bomb craters appeared cutting across the countryside I pointed it out to the Major and we both cringed. The great Hanoi based novelist Bao Ninh may have been writing about one of these craters in his international bestseller *The Sorrow of War*. He tells of a North Vietnamese soldier who promises help for a wounded enemy ARVN soldier stranded in a bomb crater. Before the soldier from the North gets back to the crater with help, it has filled with water. The soldier is lost, and the North Vietnamese soldier is tormented by the moans of the victim for the rest of his life.

We landed and quickly left the disgusting smells of the hot meals that consisted of leftover commodities from the States that had been supplied at an exorbitant profit by politically connected middlemen. As Marine General Smedley Butler said in his book *War is a Racket*! Yes, that is the name of the book and it is what he said.

Joe still had no idea why I had rushed him back to Ben Luc, but that didn't stop him from leading us straight to Ba and her lovely daughter. Soon we were all three sitting at her small counter and sucking down the noodles in her delicious traditional Pho. She used broth that she made just once a week by boiling some of the less desirable beef parts for hours. For our order she ladled hot broth into our cups and topped them with fresh sliced onions, parsley and cabbage with small chunks of a delicate white fish. Her secret was to use plenty of spices in the broth. Cardamom and ginger seemed to be the subtle stars.

As we walked on toward the pharmacy where we hoped to find Muy Ba, Joe sucked contentedly on a stalk of sugarcane and the Major, whom we called Peanut Butter, gawked at the unusual but wonderful sights. He clearly needed to get off the base more often! He asked awestruck about the outhouse perched over the fishpond. "They eat the fish?"

"Sure," I said. Where do you think Ba got the fish for your pho?"

He shook his head as we walked on towards the river, where we found several boys frolicking in the murky water. As a boys' smiling face emerged from the water, we noticed an old woman walking up the ramp to an outhouse perched over the water nearby. Peanut Butter was visibly disgusted but said nothing. I decided not to tell him Joe and I had been swimming here with the boys just before I got sick and had to spend a week in the hospital.

The deep green mangroves across the river looked like they could hide an entire revolutionary army. Our reverie was snapped by four sarus cranes flying overhead about 50 feet up. These magnificent birds were the tallest in the world with males topping out at about six feet. The naked heads of the adults shone a brilliant red in the morning sun and their long, pale, red legs gracefully followed. They trumpeted a loud but friendly goodbye as they passed over that made us all smile. Aldo Leopold says the young are called colts because they prance like baby horses when greeting the morning sun. These colts were smaller with teddy-bear tan feathers. The great prehistoric-looking birds liked the delta habitat so much they didn't bother to migrate. They mated for life and hung out mostly in Vietnam and Cambodia.

We couldn't see it from the pier, but downstream about 100 yards the pineapple boat bobbed and waited for the wedding party.

Heading back to the pharmacy, we passed the open-air community pavilion which also served as the neighborhood cinema. Several people were watching a movie on a small TV monitor. A lovely blue-winged leafbird landed softly on the corrugated metal roof of the building as we walked by. "Who chooses the movies?" the major wondered.

I knew that my friend the pharmacist chose them and that they were all meant to strengthen the people's commitment to socialism. Since they were in Vietnamese, the Americans usually just ignored them, but I just said, "Yeah, I wonder too."

We didn't have to wait for Muy Ba. She came running out and jumped into my arms screaming, "You came, you came, you came!" I could not hide my embarrassment but was thrilled to see her. She said, "I love you, Larry, and we are going to get married!"

I said stupidly, "When?"

"Now!"

Peanut Butter Cup said, "Holy crap, Larry! Now it all adds up!"

Joe said, "I knew you were headed for trouble as soon as you got on that crazy pineapple boat."

Muy Ba took my hand and walked me toward the back of the pharmacy as Joe and Major Peanut Butter laughed in amazement out front. I wasn't sure if I should join the laughing or just start crying. She got right down to business and asked if I had started the paperwork for her to go to the states. I assured her that I had, but said," Aren't we rushing the wedding?"

She reminded me that I would be leaving Vietnam soon and introduced me to her parents.

I said, "I'm pleased to meet you, Madame Giap," and reminded Muy Ba that I had already spent time with her father on the trip to Singapore. They didn't seem nervous at all. Who knows, maybe this was the tenth time they had been through the same charade.

After I told the Major that the general was the commander of the North Vietnamese Army as well as the Viet Cong, he said to me, "It seems incredible that just a few weeks ago General Westmoreland was here in Ben Luc awarding the Distinguished Service Medal to General Weyand and now here we are enjoying our little cease fire with the military commander of all the Communist forces in the country."

Tan Nguyen, the pharmacist, came out and greeted the guests and asked them to walk through the store to the courtyard in back. A tent had been erected for the special occasion. I mentioned to Tan that the tent looked like U.S. Army issue. He said "Sure, it is Larry. They are always available on the black market and seem to give us the most value for our money."

Back when I first lived in Ben Luc while pending court martial, I would occasionally stop at a similar tent that was set up on the road next to our rat friendly bunkers. A woman ran a small store in half the tent and slept in the back with her two toddlers. I enjoyed visiting with her even though we spoke different languages. She would put the little ones to bed and then come back and sit by me. She didn't sell beer, but her Coca Cola was fine and warm like her lovely hand that would rub inside my leg as we talked. What a wonderful country!

CHAPTER 21

Peace Comes to Ben Luc

I don't believe there was any mention of religion in the actual marriage ceremony. Tan Nguyen took Muy Ba by the hand as her parents let go of her. He placed my hand on hers as Major Fleece and Joe looked on solemnly. He, of course, spoke in Vietnamese, so I understood very little until he asked—first in French and then in English—if I would take Muy Ba as my wife. I said, "Yes." She soon said, "Yes." Then we were instructed to hug. She kissed me on the lips for the first time. I cried.

Then the party started. I thought I would be shaking hands with everyone, but instead it was more like a mad dash for the food and drinks. With drink and a barbequed pork rib in hand, Major Fleece was deep in conversation with General Giap. I heard him say something about the need for peace.

I followed Muy Ba to the street.

113

"Please showed me where you slept with friendly rat."

I took her hand and said, "Okay, I will show you."

We walked past Ba's pho stand which of course was closed since she was at the wedding. I wondered who was taking care of her little girl. Then I noticed the girl waving at us from a nearby house where an old man was sleeping in a hammock by the street.

Muy Ba pointed down the dirt road toward the pineapple boat and said, "Larry Ryan, you must carry me on boat this evening."

"Will we sleep on the boat tonight?"

"No, silly, it will be our first night and the people of Can Duoc expect us."

The road was dusty now, but in the truck tire ruts I could see water buffalo hoof prints from months ago. I was embarrassed thinking of the woman we had offended down the road. Joe and I had stopped to admire her breasts swaying as she tended her garden while wearing a silky see -through blouse. Her husband had chased Joe and me away with no fear of our rifles. If they were at the wedding, I sure hope they didn't recognize us!

We were probably a strange sight. Newlyweds are one thing, but there I was in my black leather and green canvas jungle boots, my incredibly comfortable green cotton jungle fatigues with RYAN in black letters over my left shirt pocket and U.S. ARMY over my right shirt pocket. The red patch on my left shoulder had a bolt of tropic lightning flashing gold in the middle, the insignia of the 25th Infantry Division.

Muy Ba was sweetly elegant in her grandmother's red wedding dress with the stunning yellow ao dai. She was quite a contrast to the old black-toothed betel-nut-chewing woman who passed us carrying a dong hai stick over her shoulder with buckets of water splashing at each end. Fresh fish perhaps.

"Oh look!" Muy Ba said as we approached the tent by the 2/14 base where I once lived. "That's Doctor Phan Dinh's house."

"No", I said, "That's the headquarters of the 2/14. That's where General Westmoreland recently awarded General Weyand the medal."

"I know that, silly. Doctor Phan Dinh was forced to rent it to the Americans, but they really do pay him regularly for using the house. Can we go into the house to see if it has been taken care of?"

"Well, let's go meet the commander and see what he says."

We walked through the secured entrance to the compound with just a quick introduction to the friendly Texan who was still the MP on duty. He told me the sergeant no longer visited the big tent next door and I just nodded not wanting to pursue the subject of the tent woman any longer! The last thing I wanted to do on my wedding day was to talk about past sexual exploits.

We found the Captain back from the wedding sitting at his desk in the doctor's house. I introduced Muy Ba and asked if he had enjoyed the wedding.

"I thought it was memorable and the food looked terrific," he said, "but I had to come back here to finish this damn situation report. You sure know how to fight a war in style, Ryan."

I asked if he would show us around the house since Muy Ba was a friend of the owner. "Go ahead and show her around while I get my work done. We are not allowed upstairs, but since the doctor is your friend, you can go right on up."

We looked at the fine old furniture and Muy Ba said, "It looks like your friends are taking good care of everything here. Let's go look upstairs now."

There were no signs of the American military upstairs and Muy Ba was relieved. She said the soldiers were not supposed to use the upstairs and was happy to see that it had not been damaged.

"Look! The pictures are still on the walls!"

Pointing to an old black and white photograph she said, "That's Doctor Phan Dinh at his graduation from medical school in Paris in 1930. The young man next to him is Ho Chi Minh."

It was as if Uncle Ho had blessed the meeting of Westmoreland and Weyand. The Captain downstairs was thinking his little base had not been attacked because he had secured it so well. There were apparently several reasons the Vietnamese had not attacked. The rent that went to the doctor each month had to be high on the list.

"Now you must show me the bunker where you slept with your ratty girlfriend."

"She was not my girlfriend." I insisted.

The bunker was right next to the gate.

"Why is the big machine gun pointed up the road?" She wondered.

"Because if we are attacked that's where the enemy will come from."

"I don't like it when you call the wonderful Vietnamese people the enemy. I am your wife, Larry Ryan! Also, if we were to attack, we would come from the river and certainly not from the highway. Do you have a way out of the base other than through the gate?"

"Yes, the guys have thrown a twenty-foot long plank over the concertina wire behind a bunker in the far end of the base so they can come and go as they please."

"When you were pending court martial and had the dirty job, where would you work?"

I pointed to the empty half barrels nearby that were still smoking from the morning's shit burning and thought about my old partner Private Ed Bishop with the goofy gap-toothed grin. I wondered if he had made it back to the family in New Jersey that made him smile sweetly every time he looked at their pictures that he pulled regularly from his damp, well-worn wallet.

"It seems like a silly waste of kerosene and fish food to burn the mess."

"Don't you think we should head back to our wedding?"

She laughed, squeezed my hand and pulled me forward. Walking back along the now familiar street, we communicated our euphoria silently. She fondled my hand so sweetly and insistently that tears of anticipation began to seep into my shorts. Soon we were back at the front of Mr. Nguyen's pharmacy just in time to see Ba, who was the first to leave after the Captain. We thanked her for helping with the wonderful feast and told her about seeing her daughter in the window. Ba was happy to hear that she was OK and had given us a friendly wave.

Ba wished us well and was followed to the door by Major Fleece and Joe. They thanked us for the dinner and offered a boisterous "Cheers" as they headed for the airfield carrying open bottles of 33 Beer. I had never seen the Major this happy before. He may have been feeling the beer, but he also clearly enjoyed the entire cross-cultural event, especially the peace building. We had helped him temporarily bury his longing for his family and his boat back in Virginia.

Next General and Madame Giap emerged smiling and thanking the guests for coming. They were pleased to see us at the door and the General promptly said "They will be waiting for us at Can Duoc, so we need to go."

He may well have been wondering if the informal truce Major Fleece had miraculously arranged would continue to hold. Mrs. Giap gave Tan Tan a big hug and told him to hurry home to Hanoi soon. He said "Yes, Mom." Then he and his friends hopped on their putt- putt motorcycles for the long ride back to Tay Ninh.

Captain Nguyen got back to the boat before us and greeted me like an old friend as I dutifully carried the bride onto the boat. The boat rocked a little, so I stumbled. I was helped on board by the General. I was red-faced with embarrassment, but no one seemed to notice. We eased into the current with three cheerful monkeys overhead seeming to wish us well. I sat between General Giap and Muy Ba wondering if I should now call him Dad. I decided to stick with General. "General, do you see any more hope for peace now that you have partied with the enemy?"

He smiled, "This has been an extraordinary interlude in the war we have been fighting against the French and now the Americans for most of my life. It took us one thousand years to expel the Chinese oppressors. Today, thanks to you, Joe, Major Fleece, the food and the beer, I feel there is hope for peace in my own lifetime!"

That made me happy and thoughtful as the boat raced downstream without its usual load of pineapples. The grasses here in the Plain of Reeds were as beautiful as ever. It felt to me like the war had already ended.

Suddenly reality caught up with us as we saw that both sides of the river had been defoliated with Agent Orange.

"General, why didn't you or Muy Ba say anything about this catastrophe?"

"Yes, it is sad, but they stopped before reaching the channel to Can Duoc so we can still feel safe under the forest canopy as we make our way upstream."

CHAPTER 22

Our First Night

I was relieved when Captain Nguyen slowed and maneuvered the boat into the channel, turned off the big diesel and switched to the small engine. Soon we docked and were greeted by a waiting crowd dressed in their finest clothes. They lined the path smiling, patting us and asking about the ceremony and the feast. It was a wonderful homecoming.

As we walked past Muy Ba's "secret" bathing pool she said, "Larry Ryan, we will bathe here this evening before our first night."

All I could say was "Great" as I thought about the stolen glances I had been blessed with here as I was starting to fall in love with Muy Ba and out of love with the U.S. Army. That first incredible trip down the river with her and her father seemed like it had been years ago, but it had just been a few months. The fear I had then of being caught AWOL was now just another pleasant memory of my new life with Muy Ba.

The people were gracious as they entertained our bizarre wedding party. It was clear that I was a curiosity like a hairy beast at the zoo while General Giap was held in reverential awe. With the Can Duoc reception and the bath completed, we finally found ourselves alone in our special nest. We had a roof, four walls and a door. There were no windows for us to worry about. No nosey little boys would be spying on us. I was nervous about how to proceed but at the same time I was thrilled that life had come to this. Muy Ba took charge then and said, "Now we must take off all our clothes and climb in under the sheet."

The bed was perfect. The air was warm, humid and smelled fresh and earthy like the jungle with no hint of Agent Orange. The sun was setting peacefully in the west and the village was quiet. Inside we just had a single candle burning on a small table.

I said, "Do I need to use a condom?" as I thrilled to the feel of her cool feet rubbing my leg slowly.

She just laughed. "NO, silly! G.I. just know slams-bams-thank-you-ma'ms! Now you are married man and you must learn how to be good husband. Remember when you told me about the pretty woman in front of you at the grocery store wiggling her butt as you stood behind her in the line?"

"Yes. Who could forget that?"

"Well, you didn't know it but she was using your greedy eyes for her own sexual pleasure. That happens in Hanoi only when the mens are gone."

"So why was she using me?"

"Maybe because her husband was gone but probably because he was slams bams ma'ams guy with no training in pleasuring the womans."

Holding her in my arms under the rough linen sheets filled my body and soul with ecstasy. It didn't hurt at all that she had taken the condom out of the equation.

After a few wonderful minutes of leisurely hugging and sweet, lip nibbling, she again took command. "Now you must learn to suck my nipples so I can enjoy it as much as you do." She gently moved my head to her right breast. You can lead a soldier to titty, but you can't expect him to actually know what to do with one. I did my best. She moved my head to the other breast and put a perfect bare leg over me.

I called for help.

"I need a cloth."

She covered my exuberant dick with my T- shirt and cradled my exploding balls with her sweet little hand as she whispered, "I love you, Larry Ryan, now go to sleep!"

We were up early and had breakfast at the little place where I had eaten on my first visit to Can Duoc. This time ordering was not a problem. I just sat back savoring the aromas of coffee brewing, bacon sizzling and the mesmerizing sounds of the jungle awakening as my brand-new wife did the ordering. In no time I was served a lovely plate of French toast with butter and cane sugar syrup. Sides of bacon and fresh pineapple combined to make this G.I. even more content. The pup that had barked at me before sniffed once, then licked my hand, as if he too were feeling the joy of the newlyweds. We shared the toast and pineapple, but the soft meaty bacon was all mine except for the scrap I slipped to Spot.

We walked on down to the boat where we were greeted by the General and his wife. I thought they would be riding with us back up to Ben Luc, but the plans had changed. They seemed distracted as they said goodbye. Captain Nguyen untied the boat and pushed it back into the stream. Tears ran down Madame Giap's cheeks as she waved. The General hugged her. They seemed to know that it would be a long time before they saw us again.

CHAPTER 23

USAID

We caught the morning chow chopper back to Cu Chi. The walk from the airfield to the PIO office was slow and pleasant. Joe and Major Fleece greeted us warmly and introduced us to Todd and Rich who looked up from their work just long enough to say, "Hello, congratulations."

The Major took us back to his office where we told him about our trip to Can Duoc. He then said, "Okay, so now what?"

I gathered that he was wondering where we would be living so I said, "If you don't mind, I'd like to work in Tay Ninh a few days so that Muy Ba can say goodbye to her friends before our flight to San Francisco."

"I thought you might try to take my hooch away from me." He seemed disappointed but relieved that we weren't asking for it. "Sure, we can use some more stories from Tay Ninh, so off you go and please enjoy your honeymoon!"

Tay Ninh was incredibly welcoming. Tan Tan and his crew must have spread the word about our marriage, because everyone we saw congratulated us. As we walked toward the Cao Dai Temple several friends greeted Muy Ba and wished her well with her G.I. husband. I wondered what else they said.

"Tubby Tan—we call him Tubby, so he won't be confused with my brother Tan Tan—is the one with the phosphorus grenade burn on his face. He told me about the battle where he had been injured. The grenade went off near his face because he was slow to jump away. The other sappers in his unit were slim and nimble and quick to jump when the grenade plopped down in their midst."

Our pleasant homecoming continued when we walked into the bakery. The clerk said, "Tan Tan said you'd be here soon." Tan Tan and his friends had obviously made better time on the return to Tay Ninh riding their little putt putts than we had riding in three different helicopters. The clerk offered us the room in the back where I stayed after the mistake at the brothel. I said to Muy Ba, "Maybe we should go say hello to your friend at the USAID office before we decide where to stay."

The USAID representative Carol Peterson was in her office and immediately jumped up and hugged Muy Ba and congratulated her. Good news sure travels fast around here I thought. Then Carol said, "Are you in need of more rice already?"

Muy Ba answered, "No, that last big shipment is still being distributed."

"I wish the ARVN (Army of the Republic of Vietnam) could be trusted with the rice, but every time we give them a shipment it is on the black market in Saigon the next day. In fact, I'm beginning to think just like your friend Larry. Oops, make that husband Larry! We are fighting for the wrong side in this stupid war."

Muy Ba was thrilled with her supportive words, thanked her, then without missing a beat asked if we could use her guest suite for our honeymoon.

"It just so happens we were expecting a state department inspector from Saigon, but he canceled as usual so, of course, we will be honored to have the wonderful Muy Ba and her kind-hearted PIO Larry Ryan stay here."

We had a fun-filled week in Tay Ninh. Muy Ba took me with her to say goodbye to all her friends. We went out to the Michelin Plantation and met with her sappers in the same upstairs room where Joe and I had stumbled upon a meeting Muy Ba was having that we took to be a Buddhist ceremony. We took a bus out towards Cambodia to see Tan Tan at his bakery. He was making a delivery, so we waited around and talked to the other bakers. They were happy to report that they enjoyed the wedding and they didn't seem to mind telling on Tan Tan. He had been riding his motorcycle too fast on the way back to Tay Ninh from the wedding in Ben Luc and almost got himself killed. On the outskirts of Saigon, he was leading their little putt putt convoy when a blue and yellow taxi had pulled out from the curb right in front of him. Luckily, he braked in time or he likely would have hit it broadside and gone flying over it and landed on his head. Now I knew why they had made it to Tay Ninh before us!

Once all the goodbyes were finished and command of the sapper unit had been transferred, we hopped the bus to Saigon and headed to the airport for the flight to San Francisco.

CHAPTER 24

Tan Son Nhut

The scene at the airport, Tan Son Nhut, was hectic as expected. The World Airways jet we were expecting to see had been sidelined for maintenance and we were told a Pan Am jet of the same size and approximate vintage was due momentarily from Taiwan.

The moments turned into hours. Lunch was offered by the sergeant in charge, but we declined the Army gruel and walked to the street for some pho which was almost as good as we had recently enjoyed in Ben Luc.

The plane finally arrived in the late afternoon and we were told that boarding would start soon. When boarding was about to begin the sergeant announced that the configuration of the Pan Am included first class seating. He assured us the service would be the same in both cabins. I knew the large leather seats up front would be coveted for the long trip.

He first boarded some officers and then asked if there happened to be any newlyweds present. We laughed, raised our hands and were quickly seated. We learned later that our friend Major Fleece, you remember Peanut Butter, had not just gotten our names on the manifest but had arranged priority seating. I sure was looking forward to seeing Mom and Dad back in Gary but, thanks to the good Major's kindness, I was hit with a taste of nostalgia for the Army I hadn't even left yet.

As soon as the door was closed the little tractor at the front of the plane started pulling us away from the gate and the large aluminum ladder that we had just climbed up. The jet engines started one at a time and we made our way to the runway. There were no other planes in front of us, so the pilot started the roll.

"This is the fun part Muy Ba. Just put your head back and we will be so relaxed by the end of the runway we'll soon be sleeping our way home." I sure was wrong about that. The Boeing 707 was loaded with fuel for the nonstop flight but still seemed to shoot straight up. We had been warned this was necessary to avoid being shot down. Of course, with Muy Ba on board we were safe but nobody had bothered to tell the Captain up front in the cockpit that she was General Giap's daughter so no Communist fighters in their right minds would have shot at this particular plane. Nevertheless, she squeezed most of the life out of my right hand apparently due to her fear of flying.

I asked if she'd rather sit on the aisle, but she wouldn't move. We soon leveled off at our cruising altitude. A lovely young blonde flight attendant wearing a red, white and blue scarf that was a Pan Am route map gave us each a round plastic blue and white logo bag with a white strap. It was loaded with Pan Am goodies for staying fresh on the trip: toothbrush, toothpaste and cologne. I was relieved to see the dark beauty flight attendant I had vacationed with in Taiwan was not working the flight!

"Why are these people all so nice to us?" Muy Ba asked. "You said in your bayonet training you were taught to yell kill the gook as you charged into the training man with your sword."

"The bayonet may look like a sword on the end of a rifle, but it is just a knife. In fact, we usually just walked around with them attached to our ammo belts and only fixed them in place for hand to hand combat when given the command to fix bayonets."

"Are you ignoring my question about the nigger gook word?"

"You should say racist gook word," I said, thinking how interacting with the people of Vietnam had changed me and many others. Soldiers who came home with fond memories of the people they had worked and played with for perhaps a year were going to be an important part of the antiwar effort we were about to join in Chicago.

And then, just as we hit some turbulence, the flight attendant handed Muy Ba a bouquet of Gerbera daisies as she said so the whole plane could hear her, "Congratulations on your marriage to Larry Ryan, and welcome to America."

Muy Ba thanked her and then said enthusiastically to Larry, "Thank you thank you and how did you know these flowers are my favorite from the Quang Ba Flower Market in Hanoi?

My mother took me there many times. It was near the park across the street from our house."

"They are not from me," I said, "Read the card."

She opened it and read in Vietnamese a message from her father:

"Congratulations my dear daughter.
I hope you are having a nice flight to America. I tried to get flowers for you in Ben Luc and then again in Can Duoc with no luck. I told Major Fleese about it and he offered to help. These flowers are from the south, but they are just like the ones you always liked in Hanoi.
Love Dad."

Larry smiled, "The General is a wonderful father."

"Yes, and funny too just like you."

"Why do you say that?"

"Because he made a joke when he said no luck in Luc silly!"

"That makes no sense to me because I had so much luck in Luc where I found you in the amazing pineapple boat!"

The big jet cruised along smoothly as we continued our 8,000-mile trip to California. We were served a light meal that had been prepared in Saigon. It tasted fine to me but was pretty much the same old thing. Muy Ba took a couple of bites and dozed off. I soon slept too.

CHAPTER 25

Guam

We woke to a jarring message from the cockpit. "Please be sure your seatbelts are fastened securely around you. Due to an unexpected change in our headwind we will soon be landing in Guam to refuel."

"Guam is the largest island in Micronesia. It is about 1500 miles southeast of Tokyo and about 6000 miles west of San Francisco. The native Chamorro people and culture were pretty much wiped out by the Christians in the 1600s. The surviving Chamorro culture suffered from way too much Spanish influence which was made obvious by the undue influence on society by the Catholic Church. But of course, things could get worse and they did in 1898 when as a result of the American victory in the Spanish-American War the U. S. military replaced Spain and declared the entire island a naval base. The people are told they are American citizens but because of an old law they cannot vote in general elections, including presidential elections because they are an alien race that cannot understand Anglo-Saxon laws."

"I know all that but because of some wonderful Jesuits the Catholics were not all bad. In fact, my father said we might stop here and if we did, we should go see some friends of his."

"How could we possibly find them?"

She pulled her father's letter from her bag and said, "We just need to show this letter with the address to the taxi driver."

I doubted that we would have time but said nothing to discourage her.

We had a smooth landing and taxied up to the small military terminal. We were on the Anderson Air Force base at the north end of the island.

The captain announced that we had lost our early morning landing slot in San Francisco. Then he cheerily added, "The Island is beautiful and since we will be sitting here for at least four hours I suggest you have a look around."

Now it looked like we did have time, but I was still skeptical of her plan. We deplaned and went immediately to a wall that was colorfully painted with a map of the island.

"Look, silly", she said, we are here, and the church is just here at the bottom of the base."

"What makes you think so?" I questioned.

"Look at the address," she said, "Blessed Diego Luis de San Vitores Church 884 Pale San Vitores Road Tumon Bay, Guam USA 96911-4013. And look here, Tumon Bay is right next to the south side of the airfield!"

"How could you possibly find it so fast on the big map? Have you been here before?"

"You don't lead sappers into battle without excellent map reading skills," She impressed and silenced me.

As we hopped into the last taxi in line, I was wondering if this was going to be the story of my life—the wife is right again!

When Muy Ba led the way through the massive front doors of the elegant church, we walked softly but our footsteps still echoed off the walls built of rich-looking old ifil wood. Just to the right of a fresco on the rear wall there was a small door. The fresco beautifully depicted the Assumption of the Virgin Mary in a style reminiscent of the work of the great Spanish painter, Velázquez. The door opened and a young priest walked towards us smiling pleasantly. He asked if he could help us. Muy Ba pulled out the note from her father and asked if we could see Father Joe Mulligan.

The priest was surprised at the request but said "Of course, just follow me to our living quarters where Father Joe is meditating." I was surprised that he was not praying but soon discovered why. He was young and handsome and could have passed for a Kennedy. He and Muy Ba spoke to each other like old friends and I soon learned that he was not only a fine Christian but a Communist as well. Then Father Joe said to me in what sounded like a Boston accent, "Do you mind if Muy Ba and I have a few words in private?"

"Be my guest." I attempted to be civil but wished that he had already been told about our recent marriage.

"I'll be waiting out front but don't forget we have a flight to catch."

I thought she gave me a dirty look as she turned back to Father Joe. I walked outside and sat down on the stairs below the massive doors. The salt air was calming. I thought about taking Muy Ba to Chicago where we would be far from the sea. If we could find a place to live near Lake Michigan perhaps, she could be happy.

Soon the doors opened with the ancient hinges crying out for oil. Father Joe and Muy Ba hugged and we were about to say goodbye when he offered us a ride back to the terminal in the church bus. We talked about stopping for a walk on the beach since we thought we still had a couple of hours to kill but decided to play it safe and went straight to the terminal. Father Joe talked the whole time about how much he loved the island and the people he was cheerfully ministering to.

As soon as we entered the terminal, we heard our names being called over the PA. We hurried to the departure lounge and found that it was empty. The door to the gate slammed shut as we approached. We weren't late according to the announcement the captain had made earlier, but we were beginning to sweat when the door popped back open and the blonde flight attendant yelled cheerfully, "There you are!" As she hustled us on board, she told us that soon after we left the airport our flight had been cleared for immediate departure. Everyone else had been rounded up easily, but we hadn't told anyone where we were going so they couldn't find us. If they had seen our multi-colored, horn blaring church bus leaving with crazy Father Joe at the wheel they said nothing. Soon we boarded. The engines were fired up and we were on our way. Since no ground fire was expected, we took off heading calmly into the wind.

Drinks were offered. I ordered *"Mot Coca Cola a nuoc da e mot 33."* The Vietnamese speaking attendant said they were out of 33 beer and offered a Heineken. Muy Ba had her Coke while I slowly sipped the delicious beer poured into a small plastic glass from a cold sweaty green can.

"So, what was that all about?" I finally had the courage to ask about her meeting at the church.

She answered with a serious tone, "Father Joe worked for several years at Saint Joseph Cathedral in Hanoi. The church is neo-Gothic and was built in 1886. He once took us on a wonderful tour of the old building and told us about it with such pride that I had to ask Mom later if he owned it!

Most of the masses there were read in Vietnamese by native priests, but Father Joe would give them in French, English and Latin. Thousands of believers visit on Christmas and Easter. Since so many of the believers were also Communists it was a good place for my father to meet with them. I went with him often so that I could look at the fine young priest. He once asked if I would come sometime alone but I never did even though I dreamed about it. "And then like a dream come true you showed up at the pineapple boat in Ben Luc looking just like Father Joe to me."

I wasn't sure if I should be pleased or jealous. Thinking again that I was lucky to be the one married to her, I dozed off.

I woke before her and stared at her lovely face as she dreamed. Her dream obviously soured, and she woke up looking sad and started to sob quietly. She took her arm away from my hand and said, "Mr. Ryan, I am thinking I have made a big mistake."

"What are you talking about?" Instantly depressed, I fleetingly wondered if I would ever really have Muy Ba as my wife.

Through her quiet tears she mumbled, "All the Americans are way too nice to me. Me and my Tay Ninh sappers have been killing the Americans because we want to rid our country of white colonial rule once and for all. Everything is so confusing. I miss my parents terribly. I worry about Tan Tan and his bakery and his little putt putt motorcycle. Do you understand?"

I told her that I thought I understood and reminded her that I had left my parents to go to war. Then I reminded her that we were doing what her father wanted us to do. I put my arm back on her leg, but she brushed it off again. Then she took my hand and squeezed it sweetly as she smiled up at me and said, "Thank you Larry."

CHAPTER 26

Back in the USA

We landed at the Oakland Army Base soon after waking. This was the same base that I left fifteen months earlier as an eager young patriot hoping to save the Vietnamese people from godless communism! Back then I had been fitted with nice new jungle fatigues and black leather and green canvas jungle boots. Boy oh boy did a few months at war ever make a difference for me. It was hard to imagine that I had once fallen for the pro war propaganda John Wayne had suckered a generation with in *The Green Berets*.

While waiting in a long line to get processed back into the States, Muy Ba pointed across the cavernous building to a very short line and said, "Please read that sign to me."

I read "Returning G.I.s accompanied by Vietnamese nationals report here." She was right again!

I was issued a DD214, my final Army orders. It showed that I had been honorably discharged with a Bronze Star and other medals. At the last stop in the discharge process, I was issued travelers checks for $500, my final G.I. pay.

A sharp young private lifted our bags and said, "Follow me."

I said, "I need to call home before we go anywhere." We walked with our luggage to the pay phones.

"How can I call my Mom in Indiana?" I asked him.

"Here just give me the number and I'll dial it."

Mother answered the collect call and when she heard I was in San Francisco she started crying with more joy than I thought the poor old arthritic, overweight Baptist Sunday school teacher had in her. It seemed the news from the war was so terrible that she had resigned herself to losing me. I told her that I couldn't wait to get home and introduce her to my new friend then hung up! Just like that I chickened out and didn't mention that I had done just the opposite of what she had in mind for me and married a Vietnamese girl.

The private led us outside to a waiting black limousine! "What's this?" I said excitedly to the uniformed driver. He said nothing but handed me a note that I immediately saw was signed by Major Fleece.

As we headed over the Bay Bridge to San Francisco I read the brief note to Muy Ba. "Welcome home Larry and Muy Ba. I hope you enjoy your stay at the old SW Hotel on the edge of Chinatown. I stayed there on my last visit and sipped Budweiser at the strip joint across the street. You'll find the food enjoyable and fairly priced in Chinatown so don't be shy. The simple free breakfast of toast and croissants at the hotel should suffice before you start exploring."

It was signed," fondly, B. Fleece" and made us both very happy.

We were soon at the hotel and found that it was already paid for, just like the limo. We tried to at least tip the driver, but he must have been afraid of the Major and wouldn't take it.

We entered Chinatown through the famous and easily recognized Dragons Gate. Our leisurely walk took us past the Far East restaurant and the *"hear no evil, see no evil, speak no evil"* monkey sculpture. We snacked at several different restaurants offering treats ready to go. Our favorite restaurant was called Delicious Dim Sum where naturally we had dim sum! It was so good that it reminded us of our first exotic Chinese food eating experience in Singapore.

Muy Ba learned that there was a Vietnamese district nearby. We asked a storekeeper how to get there and were told everyone knows if you want something Vietnamese you go to the Tenderloin district. We hopped a cab but soon found that we could have walked it in ten minutes. We sat down at the first street stand that offered pho. Muy Ba tasted her soup, smiled and pushed the plunger on her French press to help along her Vietnamese coffee in the making as she listened to her native language thrown around so cheerfully and so far from home. The Vietnamese at home and abroad maintain the French colonial coffee making habit. The robusta beans from Vietnam are quite bitter compared to the more common arabica beans. Sweetened condensed milk is the trick used to sweeten the brew. The press is used to push the grounds to the bottom of the carafe where they are kept while the coffee is poured.

I got bored after an hour of the Vietnamese banter and told Muy Ba I'd see her at the hotel after I did some shopping. We each had a room key with the hotel name on it. I worried that she would get lost, but she laughed and reminded me that she was the one with the map skills. Her new friend told me in English, "Don't worry G.I. I show her hotel no problem.

CHAPTER 27

Bibliohead

I started walking in the general direction of the hotel and stumbled upon Bibliohead, a small used bookstore on Gough Street. The sign out front bragged that they were "... a gem of a small store in the heart of San Francisco, helpful and friendly with an eclectic assortment from bestsellers to the oddball and hard to find." I didn't think I wanted oddball but knew that helpful would be good. As I lingered, several shoppers filed out with their new purchases. The clerk was now alone at the cash register, so I entered nervously and approached her.

She looked up at me and smiling said, "Can I help you find something in particular?"

She seemed so sincere that I blurted out that I had just gotten married and needed to read about what to do in bed with my young virgin wife.

143

As she led me to the rear of the store, she said matter of factly that my new wife was lucky to have me.

"Many young American men care only about themselves and end up being lousy lovers and partners. You can look at this section for a book that will help, but since we have no other customers, I will be pleased to offer some advice, if you like."

"Please do!" I quickly said thinking this was my lucky day.

So, San Francisco sex for newlywed men went something like this: "You need to start right off with an agreement to help each other enjoy the incredible pleasure of sex."

I felt my face turn red as she said, "Men who go with prostitutes just do a little slam-bam and wait for her to clean up the mess. She will generally not even kiss the naïve John. Her pay is the same for five minutes or an hour so naturally she encourages him to get it over with as soon as possible. Premature ejaculation is simply sexual dysfunction taught by prostitutes, pornography, whores and lesbians."

Noticing my discomfort, but pretending to ignore it she continued, "As an investment in your future happiness, why don't you let her stay a virgin while you learn together?"

I was relieved with this advice and asked how I should proceed. "Buy this book," she said. I bought the book and headed back to the hotel with a whole new take on marriage. After a relaxing hot bath, I went to bed and opened the book that was well used with a lot of underlining in red.

Muy Ba breezed into the room and started right in telling me about her thrilling visit to the Vietnamese neighborhood. She learned that the Vietnamese community in San Francisco is close knit and hopes the Americans will win the war so they can go back to reclaim their privileged status as collaborators.

"One pleasant young lady who reminded me of one of my sappers even invited me to go to church with her Sunday morning. I asked her what kind of church and she said."

"All the Vietnamese here go to the Saint Boniface Catholic Church nearby or The Holy Name of Jesus Catholic Church just over the next hill."

"But what about the Buddhists?"

"The crazy Buddhists all stayed back home dreaming that the Communists will save them. Are you Buddhist?"

"Do I look crazy? No, I am not Buddhist, but I have respect for the monks who pour gasoline over their heads and burn to death because they want the war to end."

"Since I am married to a G.I., they all assume I think like them. I'm looking forward to meeting the Vietnamese people that my father knows in Chicago. I know they will be different." Then she noticed the book. "What's that?"

I told her about my visit to the bookstore and she was excited. "Let's read it together."

CHAPTER 28

Success

We enjoyed the book and each other immensely and put the evidence laden towel in the bathtub to soak in cold water. In the morning our good cheer endured and carried us on foot to a café for breakfast. Over coffee we decided that Muy Ba would go back to the Vietnamese neighborhood and I would go to the bookstore for another "how to" manual.

The walk down Gough Street was pleasant enough, but the cool breeze did remind me of how much I loved the weather in CuChi. Bibliohead was busy, but emboldened by last night's stunning success, I walked right in and headed to the musty corner with the odd assortment of sex manuals. On my way back, yesterday's clerk broke away from her current customer, introduced herself as Judy and told me to look around and she would be with me soon. After a while, she quietly slipped up behind me and surprised me with a friendly, "How's it going?"

I told her that my wife and I had enjoyed the book together and barely hinted at our success, but she knew instantly what had happened and congratulated me. Her friendliness seemed sincere but prompted me to ask, "Why are you helping me, is it just to sell books?"

"No", she said with a smile. "I probably should have told you yesterday. My partner Suzie, she's up front with customers, and I, are attending Star King Theological Seminary in Berkeley. As seniors, a big part of our training is pastoral counseling. Since working full time and carrying a full load at the seminary is a challenge, we are combining our work with our studies. The plan is to wait for poor souls like you to show up in the sex help section and recruit them for our counseling practice assignment. The time I spent with you yesterday was recorded in my course log and counts as lab credit for the pastoral course."

"Wow, so we're guinea pigs!"

She then told me they would be holding a group therapy session that evening in the bookstore with several other vets who had recently returned from the war and we were welcome to attend. I liked Judy and appreciated her candor, so I told her it sounded good and I would talk to Muy Ba.

"Fair enough," she said as she handed me her card. "Take this book along and pay for it later if you decide to keep it."

When Muy Ba returned she found me sitting in a small upholstered chair in the corner by the window with the afternoon sun filtering in through the cream-colored sheer curtains. The new book was in my lap.

"You silly boy!" she said, "Another book. Can we read again in bed tonight?"

I said "Sure, are you kidding?" and told her about the group session.

She said "We should go, but now I want to take you to a museum I saw on my way home. That's funny," she said, "I just called our lovely little room here in the hotel, home!"

The Asian Art Museum was nearby and well worth the walk. The Yoga exhibit was in full swing and Muy Ba wanted to join in. I restrained her and when I showed her the tickets were $17 each, she took my hand and we moved on to the Mandala which featured "Cosmic Centers and Mental Maps of Himalayan Buddhism."

"It would be good to visit a museum of Asian history while we're here," I said.

"Yes, but now let's go get some mo pho."

"Do you mean more pho for lunch?"

"I hear people say mo fun and mo beer so why can't I say mo pho? Besides it rhymes. Mo pho sounds mo better."

She was right of course so we headed back to the Vietnamese neighborhood for pho. Unfortunately, while listening to a very happy Muy Ba chatter with her new friends in Vietnamese, I heard several women ask for mo pho. We left the mo pho restaurant and walked down to Fisherman's Wharf. There we had some touristy but tasty fried shrimp. "I like Chinatown shrimp better," she said.

She had a map and used it to get us back to our hotel riding the cable cars. The San Francisco cable cars are special. They were the first in the world and now they were the only cable cars in operation in the world. They were powered by a cable that moved continuously just beneath the street. The cable was powered by an engine in a remote location. A gripman on each car started and stopped by grabbing and releasing the cable with a long lever.

We were early for our group session but a sign on the door with our names on it said come in.

The others were probably as eager for the session to start as we were. They were already sitting in a circle in the back of the store. We sat down and watched Judy walk to the front and lock the door.

"Now, it's time to go to work. Who wants to start tonight?"

"No, no," she said. "We have new people, so we need to introduce ourselves. I'll go first then we can talk around the circle with short introductions or let it all out if you are so inclined."

Judy seemed determined to let at least a lot out as she said, "Suzie and I fell in love while working together at the Blue Moon Spa on Powell Street a few years ago. At the time it was the most respected, if that's the right word, brothel in the city. We were young, some said beautiful, and had both run away from home in the Midwest. To put it bluntly, our born-again Christian parents forced us out because we were becoming more and more obvious about our sexual orientation. The spa owners were always generous with us and monitored the rooms to be sure the customers were well behaved as far as our wellbeing was concerned."

I noticed that the vet named Bill looked especially nervous. His hands were rapidly moving from behind his head to his knees then to his lap where he balled them into fists.

"Wait a fucking minute!" Bill said as he jumped up from his metal folding chair knocking it to the floor.

I thought he was about to get violent, but Judy jumped right up with a big smile and said, "Bill, I sure was hoping someone would ask a question at this point. It's so good to see that you are wide awake. You do have a question I hope."

Bill sat down meekly and said, "Sorry, I just find it hard to believe you and Suzie worked as prostitutes and now we are supposed to open our souls to you, what gives?"

"What gives," Judy said, "is that what I said is absolutely true. As a matter of fact, prostitution comes easily for lesbians on the run as we were. Since we have no sexual attraction to the johns, the actual act is mere mechanics though certainly distasteful. After every unsavory encounter we would retreat to the girls lounge and tell the others how it went. It always amazed us that the guys fell for our bullshit."

"Like what?" Bill asked.

"My favorite was to look at a mousy old john's itsy-bitsy dick and say you're so big! The bigger I said it was the bigger the tips. You know we call it working tricks. Well the real trick was to get it over with in five minutes or less. Some of the guys were such basket cases that as soon as I sat down next to them and brushed against them as I removed my blouse and bra, they would come all over themselves and start crying. I thought give me a break, I should charge for counseling. So here we are, and I see I talked too much as usual. So, who wants to go next?"

Suzie was through closing out the day at the cash register and walked over with a smirk on her face as she unconsciously unbuttoned her stunning rose-colored silk blouse enough to reveal pure white cleavage which got everyone's attention. "We happen to have a lot more stories from the spa, would you like to hear some more of them?"

Nobody responded so *Muy Ba* introduced herself and said, "Thank you Judy and Suzie. Larry and I just got married and we are here because Larry wants to be a good husband. While he was in Vietnam, he went with beau coups slam bam thank you mam womens who said he was so big, He never learned how to pleasure the womans."

Everyone waited for her to say more but that was it.

Judy then said, "OK Larry, your turn."

"Well she must be right because she's my wife and she's always right!"

Bill shook his head and said, "I can't fuckin' believe this shit.

I have only been home from Nam for six months and I have already disappointed every miserable cunt I've been close to. Muy Ba's words obviously struck a chord with Bill who was thinking about all the bad sex he had experienced in three P alley as they called it. Pay the P, pull it out-get sucked and get back to your hooch.

Next a guy named Jerry stood up and said, "Judy, I know you mean well but there is no way I can handle group therapy so I'm getting out of here while I can still breathe."

He walked to the front and Judy, looking the part of the librarian she once dreamed of becoming, walked along and apologized to him. He said, "No need to apologize. That was all just way too real and too much for me to handle. Can I give you a call and maybe arrange a private session?"

CHAPTER 29

Serious Therapy

Judy handed him a card and said, "Please call soon," as she let him out the front door.

The next morning Jerry looked at the business card Judy had given him. The card didn't mention the bookstore. It boldly stated, "Sexual Dysfunction Counseling." He was now pretty sure this was what he needed so he called the bookstore. He was relieved when Judy answered cheerfully.

"Hi this is Jerry and I'm ready for that private session you suggested at the group session last night and I wonder how much it will cost." he blurted.

"We have a sliding scale depending on the veteran's income, so you don't need to worry about it. If you can spare $10 for tonight that will be fine. We will be taking Muy Ba and Larry Ryan to the airport this evening in the seminary's limo and would like you to join us so we can get your private session started on the way back here.

You will not need a condom, but ejaculation will be part of your first session so please save your strength for this evening."

Jerry liked the sound of the plan and knew exactly what she meant when she said, "Save your strength."

Judy's next call was to me. She asked if we would like a lift to the airport. She knew that our flight for Chicago was leaving in the evening. I told her that would be great and we agreed to meet at the bookstore.

On the way to the airport Jerry soon realized that Judy was giving him a show. There was not much conversation in the limo, but Judy was close to him and facing him. Her little jump seat didn't seem very comfortable and she moved around a lot. Soon her pale white legs were showing all the way up to her black lace panties. Curly blonde hair peeked out and Jerry was already beginning to grow as the limo pulled up to the American Airlines departure doors.

I saw those wonderful legs as well and my mind skipped back to Gary and the girl I had been so in love with right after college. She lived with her father and two sisters. Her father had a Triumph sports car and he was impressed with the little red MGA that I showed up with for my first date with Caroline. At that time, I was still a virgin and resisted Caroline's attempts to get us into a love motel. Being perpetually short of money may have saved me from an early marriage to a wonderful white girl!

As sweet and wonderful as her kisses had been, I ended the relationship at home alone and in tears after learning from a former friend that she had been married for a while during her senior year in high school. I have certainly never thanked him for the cruel gossip.

The doors popped open ending the white girl daydream and Muy Ba and I grabbed our bags and headed into the terminal.

The limo pulled away and Judy reached up and pulled down the privacy curtain so James would not be distracted from his driving chore by the therapy session.

Jerry started to sprawl in the big back seat, but Suzy and Judy plopped beside him and began their lovemaking show with him in the middle.

Judy said, "Don't worry, Jerry, we are not really going to make love. We just need to keep you erect for the sake of your therapy."

As they kissed and fondled, with him gleefully stuck in the middle, Jerry wondered about the seminary they attended. They had said it was Unitarian and he wondered if that was some cult that had popped up in California while he was in Vietnam.

The next time Judy told him no no for scratching his crotch he asked,"Are you guys Christians or just some kind of weird cult?"

Suzy squeezed Judy's lovely young thigh as she answered, "Of course we are Christians. We are also atheists."

"That just sounds like more bullshit." Jerry complained but not sounding too put off.

Suzy continued reading from the preface of *Singing the Living Tradition* within our congregations and in society at large:

"The goal of world community with peace, liberty and justice for all;
Respect for the "Our covenant as Unitarians is to affirm and promote:
The inherent worth and dignity of every person;

Justice, equality and compassion in human relations;
Acceptance of one another and encouragement to
spiritual growth in our congregations;
A free and responsible search for truth and meaning;
The right of conscience and the use of the democratic
process interdependent web of all existence of which we
are a part." from Singing The Living Tradition UUA
preface."

So, Jerry said, "Can you say that again? No, no, just kidding but I didn't hear any Christian dogma that I'm familiar with."

"Well our congregations have great respect for the words of Christ. In many cases we have paintings of him hanging on our walls along with other Unitarian saints such as The Buddha, Mahatma Gandhi, Doctor Martin Luther King and Sojourner Truth."

Jerry said, "I do like the spiritual growth part," as he looked down at his crotch.

Soon they were back at the bookstore. Judy hopped out first and thanked James for the ride.

Suzy said to Jerry, "Let's wait here until the crowd on the sidewalk moves on. If your hell-bent for pussy tent pole burst through your jeans, the cops would probably be here in seconds."

Once inside Judy made sure the door was locked and the *Closed* sign in place, then led them back to the door discreetly marked *Therapy Room.*

Jerry stood there amazed at the beauty of the smooth silk covered bed that dominated the room. Judy lit some exotic smelling candles and told him to wait until she and Suzy had removed their clothes.

They stood one on each side of the bed and made a practiced show of removing their clothes in unison. Jerry stood in awe as first their blouses came off followed by each showing one sweet tit and then the next as he nearly swooned. With the preliminaries out of the way, Judy told him to undress and lay face down in the middle of the bed. He had a strong back and perfect ass, but it didn't faze the therapists. They proceeded as planned.

The feathers were taken from the tables and the Marin County feather dance about drove Jerry to the brink for the tenth time today.

Jerry was told that he should fondle the women for the next 15 minutes and then masturbate.

When the timer went off Judy asked him how long it would take him. "Oh, about ten seconds as ready as I am," he said.

Judy said, "If you finish in less than five minutes, we'll give you free conjugal therapy service for a month."

"No problem." Jerry said.

Instead of the easy win he was expecting he started to flag after three minutes.

Judy and Suzy said in unison, "That's enough."

Before he could get depressed over his loss, Judy reverted to her professional voice and said, "Now you have completed the first and most important part of your therapy. For most of the four hours before you were told to masturbate, we kept you hard and eager. The lesson here is that foreplay is also important for any male partner in a relationship. You never experienced anything like that before because you were either with hookers or you rushed it with your dates because you were trained in the brothels of southeast Asia. If you would like to come back tomorrow and practice using a condom, we would love to see you."

Suzy added cheerfully, "We like you, Jerry. We think the healing process will go well for you. So, go on about your life until tomorrow at 5 p.m., then come back for some well-deserved success in bed."

CHAPTER 30

Unitarian Counseling

Perhaps you have been wondering what happened to our heroes. On their flight to Chicago Muy Ba slept with a smile on her face and Larry daydreamed about a plane crash where the two of them were the only survivors. They floated down on a wing and jumped into a big tree at the last second. Falling through the branches slowed them. When they hit the soft bed of pine needle duff on the ground, they were knocked unconscious. They woke up under the tree unable to breathe, because all the air had been forced out of their lungs. After a few seconds of fear Larry began to breathe and then woke up.

They were met at the airport by Dr. John LeDuc, a friend of General Giap who had come to the States in 1954 after the victory over the French at Dien Bien Phu. He took them straight to what was now Larry and Muy

Ba's house on North Seminary Avenue. The house had been paid for in cash because no mortgages were available in the redlined neighborhood. Redlined meant the banks and nearby DePaul University had an informal agreement with some realtors to push down the value of the local housing stock so it could be purchased by them in a few years for a song.

It was a two flat and the upstairs apartment had already been rented to Bill Ayers and Bernardine Dohrn, a young couple in hiding from the FBI because of their antiwar actions. Larry wondered why the name at the 2nd floor doorbell sounded Filipino. "Oh, the Filipinos come often to use the washer and dryer in the basement and to get their mail. The real tenants just come at night, so all the neighbors think it's just the Filipinos living here," the doctor said. Muy Ba said, "I look forward to meeting them all."

Doctor John, as he preferred to be called, helped them open checking and saving accounts at The First National Bank on Lincoln Avenue. I was surprised to see that the savings account was opened with $50,000 and the checking with $10,000. "What's all that money for?" I asked.

Doctor John said, "I'm not sure and I don't even really know where it came from, but you can use it however you see fit. You can trust your upstairs neighbors if they need money and you will need money to visit contacts in New York and Paris."

That sure shut Larry up but Muy Ba could see that it made him nervous. "Is that a lot of money?" she asked him.

"It sure is."

"Since my father and Doctor John want it in our account, I know it's ok, but that doesn't mean you can use it to go to Las Vegas and practice some silly cards games!"

Lost in Vietnam

CHAPTER 31

Die Gedanken Sind Frei

While walking around the neighborhood killing time Sunday afternoon, Jerry stopped to listen to some familiar music coming from the open front door of a church on Cathedral Hill. They were obviously singing an old favorite:

"Die Gedanken sind frei my thoughts freely flower
Die Gedanken sind frei my thoughts give me power
No scholar can map them
No hunter can trap them, no one can deny
Die Gedanken sind frei!"

He remembered visits to Grandma Gerde's house where it seemed she was always baking cookies and singing that song. He decided to stop in some Sunday for a service and then he noticed that it was Unitarian.

He knew that Grandma referred to herself as a freethinker and marveled at the connection to the wonderful women at the bookstore.

Finally, it was 5pm Monday and Jerry was at the front door of the bookstore looking at the closed sign. He checked his watch and then tried the door, which was unlocked. He stepped in and was about to lock up when he noticed an old lady back at the knitting shelf. He said hello and asked if he could help her.

"Well no, young man, I'm just thinking about buying this musty old Elizabeth Zimmerman book of classic knitting patterns. Don't you think this sweater would be perfect for my two-year-old grandson?"

"I'm sorry but the store is closed and the cash register tape for the day has already been run." He noticed her smile slip a bit and said, "But you can take it with you and pay for it next time you're in, or just return it if you like."

"Oh, thank you so much."

Jerry locked up and headed back to the ROOM! He wondered if he'd be in trouble for being late but was greeted with smiles, hugs and kisses.

He started to tell them about the old lady out front but, Judy stopped him saying, "We watched you on the closed circuit, you were terrific! In fact, you're hired!"

Jerry wasn't sure he wanted to be hired-whatever that meant-but he was cheered by their cheerful reaction.

"She's a friend from church and comes in often looking for some lost and lonely soldier to replace her granddaughter Sally's husband. He had come home in a body bag a few months ago. He was such a handsome young man. Black, like most who come home dead. Only 12 percent of the population is black but most of the KIA's are black. It is just not fair."

Judy went on to say, "Her grandson is named Emmett after Emmett Till who was murdered by a white mob in Mississippi probably because he looked so nice that a young white woman had flirted with him. He was brutally lynched at age 14. The barb wire that was around his neck is now on display at the Emmett Till museum in Glendora, Mississippi. "

Jerry said, "Well, I'm sure not a soldier anymore and don't feel lonely at all now that I've discovered the world's best bookstore but what about the granddaughter? Do you think I should try to help out?"

"Now that's an interesting take on a possible blind date. Sally is a gorgeous young mom but certainly not in need of a sympathy fuck if that's what you're thinking."

Jerry was taken aback. "I'm sorry it sounded like that to you. The possibility of a date arranged by my new bookstore connection is intriguing and exciting! Where do I sign up?"

"Hold on baby! Not so fast. Our rule is no dates arranged here until our clients are ready."

"I'm ready!"

"Not until you graduate from the ROOM," she said pointing to the back.

With a pleasant sensation in his crotch he headed to the room in back.

CHAPTER 32

Chicago

We were soon comfortable in our house on Seminary Avenue in Chicago. The Filipino nurses were always friendly and came most every day to use the washer and dryer in our basement. On more than one occasion they held parties in the upstairs apartment and always invited us. This may have been just so we wouldn't complain about the party noise, but we loved the garlic laden dishes that graced the dining room table. My favorite Filipino dish will always be adobo, pork braised in garlic, vinegar, oil and soy sauce. The nurses served it at all their wonderful parties.

Now and then I would be asked to help with the hot water heater or the heat in the apartment. The thermostat for the hot water heat for the whole house was located by a south facing window upstairs. The Filipinos liked to keep that window wide open in the wintertime to air out the place after their parties. That would send the heat in our apartment skyrocketing so I would go up and explain how it worked to Marcus, the civil engineer who had signed the lease. He never got it, or just ignored my requests, so I clipped the wires and installed a new thermostat in our apartment. We now controlled all the heat. One day I was chatting with him near the now useless thermostat and he pointed at it and dismissively said it was broken. They learned to live with less fresh air! Just the same we continued to enjoy the big parties they threw for the entire four years we lived together.

Once while I was working on the hot water heater in the basement Esmeralda arrived with a basket of laundry. She started some of it in the washer and was working at some stains with an old washboard in the laundry tubs. I walked over when I finished with the water heater and told her it should work much better now that I had removed several inches of accumulated rust particles from the bottom of the tank. She then asked how we had liked the last party. I noticed that her top blouse buttons were open, and she was offering a wonderful view of young Asian bouncing tits as she rubbed up and down on the board. Her generous offer was ignored with difficulty and I headed back upstairs to Muy Ba with my happy Johnson looking for action.

The neighbors on either side and across the street were friendly as well. When a strong wind knocked down a diseased locust tree to the north, old Joey saw me working on it and with an old country God bless offered to split the cost of removal. He didn't see me pick up the downed power line or he would have thought I was crazy. Lucky for me it was not hot.

To the south of us a young newlywed would always greet me with a sexy smile. One day she was holding an adorable puppy against her braless boobs. I asked if I could hold it. As I gently and slowly lifted it I could feel her nipples harden through her skimpy tee shirt. Again I hurried back to Muy Ba who asked where I got all my "Energies!"

When the Filipinos left for the day and the antiwar activists showed up in the evening, the smells gradually moved from the heartwarming smells of roasting garlic to the sweet excitement of burning grass.

We soon learned over a wonderful dinner of dumpster diver delights that Bill and Bernadine were leaders in the faction of the Students for a Democratic Society called the Weathermen. The more staid SDS was willing to let the war against Vietnam rage while they stayed out of jail and acceptable to the mainstream antiwar movement.

I soon had a taste of jail myself and Muy Ba and I agreed that sticking with the mainstreamers and out of jail would be best for us. I had celebrated Lyndon Johnson's announcement that he would not seek reelection with margaritas at Butch McGuire's, a fine pub on Division street. On my way home a grouchy cop stopped me at the corner of Clark and Fullerton. The big red Plymouth was festooned with Eugene McCarthy campaign signs including a big triangular pizza delivery type sign on the roof so of course he knew I was a Commie! I insisted that I hadn't been speeding and refused to let him take my license in place of arresting me. I held on to him to save him from hitting me illegally and ten of his buddies came along and had a party beating on me with their nightsticks and leather covered brass knuckles. They temporarily blinded me with Mace.

I got a terrific reception from other guests at the Cook County Jail. The word got out, mistaken luckily, that

I had killed a cop, so I was treated like royalty even though I hadn't even hit him. A very crooked leach lawyer called my mother and talked her out of $500 because I had supposedly killed a cop. I then gave $300 to a lawyer friend of a friend who just told me to plead guilty and get it over with. I ended up following the advice of the court appointed no charge attorney. He had me plead guilty and pay the first cop a bribe of $300 which was said to be to replace his damaged uniform. I was released and the arrest was erased from the record. I immediately stopped payment on the illegal bribe. When I showed up a month later at traffic court there was the damn cop again. I was told by the prosecutor that I could pay the cop the $300 cash and the drunk driving charge would be waived. I told the judge that I would only pay in open court. He said to go ahead and pay. Anytime I think of the words I mouthed to the asshole as I counted out the money I smile.

When I got home Muy Ba said she wasn't worried because my mother had called her and said I was OK. Which reminds me, Muy Ba still laughs when she remembers being introduced to my mother. I said, "Hi Mom, I'd like you to meet Muy Ba."

Mom's response was "We don't drink." You'll hear more about Mom's drinking soon.

A few years later Dad was forced to retire early because of heart trouble. They bought a house trailer in a park full of white Mexican haters in Brownsville, Texas. We wondered why they chose Brownsville instead of central Florida where they had vacationed for many years. Eventually we learned they chose a Mexican border town so Mother could get pills for her arthritis that her Indiana doctor would not prescribe. After twenty years of the suspect cortisone pills, she finally ran out and was shocked the pain did not return. She wondered how many years she had taken the drug after her cure and how much bone loss she suffered needlessly. We would visit every winter and take them to a wonderful night club across the border in Matamoros after a stop at the pharmacy. The club was called The Drive In. The music was mellow. The margaritas were so smooth Mother downed them like lemonade and Dad loved the fresh Bohemia beer which was served with bowl after bowl of hot salty redskin peanuts. They liked it so much one night they talked about the dance where they had met 50 years earlier in Emily, Minnesota. Dad even remarked that Mom looked so good that night dancing without a bra that he couldn't resist her. Lucky for me he married her. I cherish the photo of them in front of the place posing on Dads Indian motorcycle.

The author and a friend on lunch break.

The street as seen from the Majestic Hotel in Saigon.

The author and a friend at the Saigon Zoo.

The Continental Palace in downtown colonial Saigon
where Graham Greene stayed in Room 214 while
writing "The Quiet American."

Outside the Continental Palace, 1967.

Houseboat on the Saigon River.

The author at the Saigon Zoo, 1967.

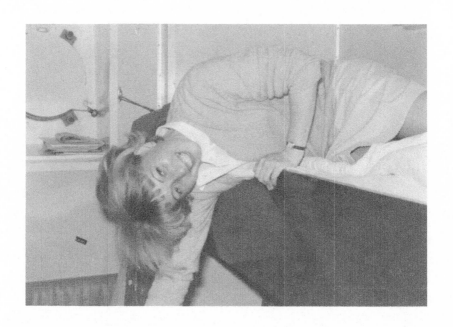

The striking blonde.

Water lilies at the Saigon Zoo.

American occupied Saigon, 1967.

Shaded walk at the Saigon Zoo.

Pagoda at Saigon Zoo.

The Mekong River in Ben Luc.

The Continental Palace where the author met
"the striking blonde" in 1967.

The author at the Cao Dai Temple in Tay Ninh.

A street scene in Saigon.

25th INF Division helicopter.

Fishing in Ben Luc.

A view of China during an AWOL visit.

Another view of China.

1st Prize
Division Photo Contest

A tank from the 3rd Squadron, 4th Cavalry guards Highway 1 between Cu Chi and Saigon. The original of this winning entry in the first Combat Photography Contest is a 35mm color slide. Photo is by PFC Lawrence A. Craig of Headquarters and Headquarters Company, 1st Brigade.

The author and a friend in Hong Kong.

CHAPTER 33

Weatherman

Doctor Le Chan stopped by our Chicago house often. He had become attached to Vietnamese coffee made the French way. He showed up once smiling broadly with a box gift wrapped for Muy Ba. She was pleased to see a French coffee press inside. They had all the ingredients and were soon pressing hot condensed milk through the ground coffee.

After a while the Doctor said to Muy Ba, "Your father wants to know what your plans are for continuing your education."

The coffee was pleasant, the moss roses were pretty along the black steel fence in front of the house but just the same Muy Ba said, "Why doesn't Dad just write to me and why doesn't he tell us what Tan Tan is doing in Tay Ninh?"

The Doctor said apologetically, "We have worked hard to insulate you from possible detection as an enemy agent. It is absolutely impossible for you to receive mail directly from Hanoi. I will write clandestinely to the General this evening and tell him about our discussion about your education and will be sure to ask about Tan Tan."

Muy Ba was still not pleased. She said, "I'm here to fight for peace, not to better my education."

He said, "Of course I understand how you feel but I have arranged an interview for you with the chair of the Department of Ethnic Studies at DePaul. We can walk there in five minutes."

The Chair was a nun. She complimented Muy Ba on her excellent English and expressed heartfelt regret for the war against her country. Muy Ba was surprised when the lovely nun suggested that a PhD program in Russian literature at the University of Chicago would probably be a better fit for her since she was fluent in Russian and had already read many of the Russian masterpieces. In fact, she was currently reading Fathers and Sons by Turgenev which she held in her hand.

"Where is that university?" she asked now feeling a little trapped.

"It is on the South side." the doctor answered, "The train you can catch just around the corner on Fullerton will take you right there with just one change of trains in the loop."

"I'll try to make an appointment for you for tomorrow. Can I come again for coffee?"

"Don't you ever work?" she said and quickly added, "Please come again for coffee but not before seven o'clock."

I joined Bill Ayers for a nice breakfast of soft bacon, crispy hash browns and eggs over easy with whole wheat toast. Bill had ordered the same breakfast. We were at the Seminary Restaurant at the intersection of Lincoln Avenue, Halsted Street and Fullerton, two blocks from home. I was still nervous about the $50,000 so quickly told about the money and the suggestion from Doctor Le Chan that the money be shared. Bill said, "No No! If the Feds found out that we were being funded by the North Vietnamese, our credibility would tank overnight."

Bill switched to the current agenda and asked "Would you and Muy Ba like to join our group for a walk down Seminary Avenue tomorrow with Bobby Kennedy and Cesar Chavez?

"Of course!" I said, "Unless you guys have some violence in mind."

"We will walk along with them singing *We Shall Overcome* and will join the BOYCOTT GRAPES chants but at some point, we will hand out our antiwar cards and chant a little 'Ho Ho Ho Chi Minh, The NLF is Gonna Win!'"

"Terrific, you can count on us."

The next morning Doctor Le Chan arrived bright and smiling at about 9:00. "We have an appointment at the University of Chicago!" he exclaimed.

"But my friends tell me it is owned by Standard Oil," said Muy Ba. "I would rather study with the nice nun at DePaul and I could walk to school just like I did in Hanoi."

"Well those dirty capitalists have the best university between New York and California, and I promise you will enjoy the train ride." "And besides," he continued, "I knew you would wonder so I checked the school's history. It was founded in 1890 by the American Baptist Education

Society and oil magnate John D. Rockefeller. The University's land was donated by Marshall Field, owner of the legendary Chicago department store that bore his name. Rockefeller described the donation as the best investment he ever made."

Doctor LeDuc and Muy Ba walked the two blocks to the train station by the library. The Doctor bought their tickets and they walked through the seven-foot-tall kid proof turnstile and up 75 well-worn wooden stairs to the sunny platform. A train was just pulling out, but another was due in ten minutes. The ride to the University on the Red Line took just 58 minutes and they did not have to change trains. The backs of the tenements that faced the train as they flew by fascinated Muy Ba and then suddenly they left the elevated tracks and were underground in the subway racing south to the loop. The train stopped and as several passengers got off and more boarded, Muy Ba looked at the pretty porcelain tiles that announced State Street exit, Monroe Street exit and Marshall Fields.

"Was the Marshall a great soldier?" she asked as the train accelerated towards the South Side. Field Marshall Rommel of North African fame was clearly on her mind. She was now totally confused. "How could this Field Marshall have the best store in Chicago with its own train stop and own the university as well?"

Her interview went well and she was accepted into the program. The news that she could do much of the work from home and use the nearby DePaul University library cheered her.

CHAPTER 34

Marshall Field

My Chicago vacation days were over. I had to find a job. I worked with a headhunter who sent me on several interviews for industrial sales jobs which yielded zip. Next, he said let's try medical. The smartass armchair warrior from Johnson and Johnson who interviewed me sent word back that I was shell shocked. Imagine that— soldier returns from war and talks about it! Next, I needed to go to the northern suburb of Skokie so my mother drove me. Mother drove in often in those days from Indiana to help us get settled. Muy Ba tagged along and entertained Mom with stories of growing up in Hanoi.

I managed to keep a lid on the war stories and got the job with Parke Davis. I was given a big red Plymouth company car and told to park it in the Grant Park underground lot. I walked my territory around the loop and kept my drug samples in a closet sized room in the Marshall Field annex. The rent for the room was $12 a month. I started my sales calls with "Hi, I'm Larry Ryan, your new Parke Davis man and I just got back from the war in Vietnam."

I went on to tell the pharmacists and physicians we were fighting for the wrong side in the war. My honesty was rewarded with unusually good sales. No one before me had ever sold so many vitamins and generated so many prescriptions in this Chicago Loop territory.

When the company decided to stop selling amphetamines, or speed as it is commonly known, pharmacists were told to return their speed supplies to me and I was instructed to discard them.

My mother was pleased with my new job because I always had gifts for the customers and shared them with her. She liked the pens and the diamond cut fingernail files, but the sleeping pills were her favorites. My baby brother Daniel, four years my junior, made the trip from Indiana to visit often. I wondered why until I discovered that he had been supplying various barflies with birth control pills from my sample supply.

I found a much more satisfying use for my samples. The Black Panther party had an office on west Madison Avenue, just eight blocks from the closet in the Marshall Field annex where I kept my samples. I soon became a regular at the Panther office. My first walk up the steep stairs behind the steel reinforced door was an eye opener. I was dressed in a business suit complete with necktie, pink cheeks and a nervous smile. I was greeted by a beautiful young militant at least six foot six with an afro and a black beret.

"Can I help you?" he said.

"I'm a Parke Davis salesman and I wonder if you'd like free samples for your clinic?"

"Right on brother! Come on up and talk to Doc Satchel."

Ronald, Doc Satchel, was the minister of health for the Chicago Black Panther Party at the time. "Good to see you or am I just dreaming? We need everything you got but how do you happen to want to help?"

"The doctors' offices that I'm supposed to sell to don't seem to need them and I know you will make good use of them. Some of the pharmacists will buy them if I clean off the word sample on each capsule with a Q Tip and rubbing alcohol."

I told him that I felt just like him that healthcare should be a right and not a privilege.

"The medical profession within this capitalist society is composed generally of people working for their own benefit and advancement rather than the caring aspects of medicine. Poor people in general and black people in particular are not given the best care available. Our people are treated like animals, experimented on and made to wait long hours in dingy waiting rooms."

"What do you have there?" he said, pointing at the box under my arm.

"Just Ponstel for pain, but I can order any free samples you want if Parke Davis makes them."

I was later able to make a few deliveries to Doc, mostly antibiotics and birth control pills, before the Federal Government working with Cook County sheriffs and the Chicago Police murdered Mark Clark and Fred Hampton as they lie unarmed face down in bed. After a lot of gunfire with all rounds except one determined to have been fired into the apartment, two Chicago cops went into the bedroom and executed the men in bed. In a civil suit it was found that the cops manufactured evidence and the families and surviving Panthers were awarded $1.8 million.

The Huffington Post referred to the killings as nothing but a northern lynching. In his blog on February 3, 2003, G Flint Taylor reports that when Fred was twenty-one, he escorted him into the venerable Lincoln Hall at Northwestern University to address the student body.

"He was only 21 years old, but he captivated the audience, as he always did, with his dynamic and analytical speaking skill, a mixture of Malcolm X, Dr King and Lupe Fiasco. It was his unique leadership, together with the revolutionary politics he so convincingly espoused that made him a target of law enforcement."

Black Panther Party member Bobby Rush survived the attack and went on to serve in Congress as the representative of Chicago's First Congressional District where he has repeatedly been elected since 1992. The voters choose the former Panther every time they get a chance.

CHAPTER 35

Acapulco

With Muy Ba buried in reading for grad school, brother Daniel and I decided to use the speed pills and big red Plymouth for a quick run to Acapulco, Mexico. I had been there a few years before. Back then I had a little red MGA sports car convertible. My friend Tom Malcolm and I had some time off between jobs and decided it was time for some adventure. My father and I had just finished rebuilding the engine. Dad discovered that the reason for the engine trouble was a supercharger made of aluminum. He advised me not to use it. But with the supercharger engaged, the car ran like lightning so I could not resist.

We got as far as Joplin, Missouri, before the head gasket blew. With the head removed it was obvious that we had burned up the head by driving with the blown gasket. The garage tracked down another head for us at a junkyard in Kansas City. A very cheap hotel became home as we waited for the part. Back on the road again, we were careful to tighten the head nuts two or three more times over the next several days to be sure we didn't blow another gasket.

Our trip would have been even quicker if we hadn't been stuck at the border for an hour while a Mexican customs agent harangued us about the need for a power-of-attorney to take the company car into Mexico. He finally gave up on us and we were on our way. We decided that he was right about the need for papers but was hoping we would try to bribe him to ignore it.

A pair of lovely young stewardesses latched on to us near the beach where we found them cowering in the shade with sunburns and suitcases. We took them back to our quaint, charming and inexpensive hotel across a parking lot behind the Hotel Presidente which was on the beach. We had separate rooms luckily. Our doors opened onto a balcony that ran the full length of the hotel. The gentle sea breezes wafted through the fronds suggesting a taste of paradise. The owners were an American couple from Arizona. She managed the hotel while he did what he had done as a professor at Arizona State University. He took tourists on nature treks into the desert with his Land Rover.

The flight attendants had been booted from their room at another hotel at the 11 o'clock check out time and didn't have a flight home until 8 p.m. I eased their pain with some fast-acting Parke Davis Ponstel pain pills. Sarah loved the aloe lotion I gently applied to her body. She said she trusted me more than her real doctor as she removed her swimsuit top and asked me to massage her tits as well even though they weren't burned! Hmm, I do wonder if it was illegal for me to practice medicine in

Mexico. We got them to their flight on time and were soon back on the beach getting way too much sun ourselves. The water was crystal clear, and the waves took us 20 feet into the air then dropped us to the pristine sandy beach.

That evening I left brother Daniel at home in the hotel and ventured up the hill to La Huerta, a famous nightclub encircled with flowering cactus, morning glories, bougainvillea in several vibrant shades of purple and red. I thought about picking a flower but noticed inch long thorns sticking along a vine with pinkish purple flowers.

I was enjoying my first bohemia along with ceviche and sliced avocado in the open-air lounge as an old fan rotated above when a lovely young brown beauty gently sat in my lap and started licking my sunburned left ear. It felt pretty good, so I pulled her to me and asked how much. She said $20 but before we could leave a guy came along with a little contraption that looked like it might have been an old telegraph machine. He had me hold two copper colored six-inch-long tubes that were connected to the box with bare electrical wires. As he slowly pulled the plunger out of the black box, I felt what was at first a pleasant sensation as a low watt current flowed into my hands. As the voltage increased, I said thanks but basta, basta. That's enough! He continued to increase the voltage as my misery intensified. I thought about Muy Ba and felt guilty until he stopped for $5. I quickly forgot about Muy Ba and headed back to Alma's room with her.

We took off our clothes and she had me lay on my back as she laved my balls with her sweet tongue. I thought about my lessons at the bookstore momentarily but as she put her sweet and delicious pointy tits in my eager mouth, I went crazy and soon realized I had slipped back into the shoddy sex of the slam bam variety.

The trip back to Chicago was fast and boring with two notable exceptions. I took speed to stay awake and Ponstel for the sunburn pain for the first shift while Daniel slept soundly in the back seat thanks to the Parke Davis sleeping pills. He awoke once as we were sliding sideways down the highway in the Sonoran mountains. I saw several campesinos jump into the brush to save themselves. Daniel awoke another time as I braked for horses running loose in the desert near Saltillo. I thought I had sideswiped a horse but saw it running away looking healthy. Daniel insisted that I hadn't hit a horse but at the next Pemex gas station I saw the damage. The right rear-view mirror was hanging by the control cable. Lucky horse and darn lucky speed freaks! We flew through customs at Nuevo Laredo, Mexico and traded places at San Antonio. Daniel's twenty-hour shift was uneventful. Our older brother had at least taught him to drive sensibly!

I dropped Daniel in Indiana and drove home on the new Chicago Skyway. Muy Ba was waiting at the front door and greeted me cheerfully, jumping up and down with her legs flying out to the side. It was heaven to be home.

She had news. The following letter had arrived while I was laying on the beach in Acapulco:

Hi Muy Ba and Larry,
We sure miss you here at the bookstore. You were our best guests and students ever!
Thanks to your help Jerry has finished his therapy and successfully dated a woman we fixed him up with.

In fact, they have gotten married and want to move to Chicago to join you in your antiwar work.

His new wife, Sally, was married to a young black soldier who came home in a body bag. Jerry is already planning to adopt her son Emmett.

With love for peace, justice and joy,

Suzy and Judy

"That is so wonderful," Larry said.

"Where will they sleep? I know, we'll ask the doctor about it," Muy Ba said.

We immediately wrote back and told Suzy and Judy we were excited about Jerry, Sally and Emmett coming. We sent driving instructions and told them to come straight to the house on Seminary.

Larry said, "Maybe this is what the money is for."

"Why not?"

The doctor agreed and we soon found an apartment for them just around the corner on Montana Street. Bill was pleased to hear reinforcements were coming from San Francisco. He was just plain elated when told they would be in an apartment nearby at 1016 West Montana.

CHAPTER 36

Jerry and Sally

The following Monday morning the doctor showed up at 9:00 for coffee. At 10:00 the Filipinos started arriving with laundry and with little Marcus Marcus in tow. That drove Bill and Bernadine downstairs. The good doctor wondered how plans were coming along with the Weathermen. Bill said, "We are expecting reinforcements soon from San Francisco that Larry and Muy Ba have recruited."

And just like that, as if on cue, the doorbell rang. Jerry was sitting on the bench on the front porch surveying the neighborhood. Emmett was shielding his eyes with his hands and looking through the sheer curtains into the living room at the thick cream-colored oriental rug. Muy Ba had fallen in love with the rug when she found it hanging on the wall in the rug department at Marshall Fields. Muy Ba opened the door and immediately gave Jerry a big friendly hug and said, "We are so happy see you! Now come in, come in."

Sally hesitated "Oh Muy Ba, I'm so happy to finally meet you, but I need a bath and I would love to put on some clean clothes before I try to visit. Jerry hasn't slept more than a few hours since we left San Francisco and he is worried about parking the car."

Doctor Le Chan said hello to Jerry then said, "Would you like to follow me to your apartment? It's just around the corner and has a parking place for you in the backyard as well." The new arrivals were soon settled in and plans were made to meet the following morning after they had caught up on their sleep.

In the morning, when Bill and Bernadine saw Larry working in the yard, they went down to discuss plans. Bill thought he and Larry should go to breakfast with Jerry. Bernadine and Muy Ba decided to offer some assistance to Sally in the new apartment. With the usual breakfast ordered at the Seminary Restaurant, Bill asked Jerry what had prompted him to come to Chicago to work with the Weathermen.

"I had heard you had something to do with bombing the Pentagon and that was the best thing I had heard since returning from the fucking war. Is that really true? Can you tell me about it?"

So, Bill told them his story.

CHAPTER 37

Bill's Story

"We pulled together a special group that scouted the Pentagon irregularly for months. When a new escalation in Vietnam became imminent, Anna, Aaron and Zeke got a storage locker outside D.C., moved some explosives in, and then found a cheap apartment nearby which they could rent for just a week. Their reconnaissance led them deep into the bowels of the Leviathan. They soon knew every hall and stairway, every cul-de-sac and office and bathroom. Everything was elaborately mapped. Their apartment began to look like an alternative war room, the dark mirror image of the Pentagon itself.

"Anna, her fingertips painted with clear nail polish to obscure the identifying marks of her naked hand, heavily disguised in suit, blouse, briefcase, dark wig and thick glasses, began entering the Pentagon every morning with hundreds of other workers. She walked the halls, ate

breakfast in the cafeteria, and left by eleven. She was never challenged. I can do it, she said finally, pulling out her sketches and maps. Here--she pointed to an isolated hallway in the basement of the Air Force section--I've been here four times, never seen another person, and there's a woman's' room halfway down, right here. She made an X on the map. There's a drain on the floor, narrow but big enough, I think, she said. One more visit was planned in order to unscrew the cover and take the dimensions of the space.

"Anna entered the Pentagon for "work" the next day at 9:00 am. She was in the chosen woman's room and the stall by 9:10 a.m. She locked the door, hung up her jacket, and pulled plastic gloves, a screwdriver, and tape measure from her briefcase. The grated cover was gunky but easy to pop off once the screws were out, and there was a comfortable 4-inch diameter drain that ran down for over a foot. Anna replaced the drain cover, wiped the area down and was back in the apartment by 10:00 am.

"A delicate and complicated series of phone calls built a consensus from all quarters to go forward. Aaron was a specialist, and Zeke assisted as he customized a sausage twelve inches long and three inches around, with a tiny timing device at one end and a suspension arm fashioned from fishing line and hook at the other. Aaron packed the thing into a briefcase below official-looking papers and personal effects. Zeke walked Anna to the train, hugged her, and went off to a bookstore for the two hours before they would meet up in a trajectory far from the target and far from home.

"When Anna appeared in the trajectory, making her way slowly down the street, Zeke's heart leapt, but he calmed himself, waited, and watched. Switchback, turn, switchback, break-away. Certain that she was safe, he

practically jumped into her arms. They were back on their block by nightfall.

"All that long day Aaron worked to close down the Washington operation, emptying the storage area, cleaning out the apartment, and paying the remaining bills. Aaron was stocky and muscular, close-mouthed but even-tempered deeply confident without a hint of arrogance. He was also the backbone of the group-- entirely committed and trustworthy, hardworking and dependable. Aaron had been an emergency room nurse and a lumberjack. A guy we all believed could survive in the Australian Outback or the Siberian wilderness for weeks with nothing but a pocketknife, or the streets of Greenwich Village with only a couple of dollars in his pocket. Aaron was smart but never showy, able to improvise when necessary--the model middle cadre.

"At eleven, Aaron pulled on plastic gloves and taped a statement about the impending attack beneath a tray in a phone booth across the street from the Washington Post offices. He then moved across town, and at eleven thirty called the Pentagon emergency number. In twenty-five minutes, a bomb will explode in the air force section of the Pentagon, he said calmly. I'm calling from the Weather Underground and believe me this is no prank. Clear the area! Get everyone out! You have twenty-five minutes. Viet Nam will win!

"He moved two blocks away and called the local police station, repeating the message. Then he moved once more to call the Post, directing the night operator to the statement in the phone booth explaining it all. Comrades in New York, Chicago, Los Angeles and San Francisco simultaneously directed local newspaper operators to copies of the statement taped neatly to nearby phone booths. And then Aaron, too, was off.

"Although the bomb that rocked the Pentagon was itsy-bitsy--weighing close to two pounds---it caused "Tens of thousands of dollars" of damage. The operation cost just under five hundred dollars, and no one was killed or even hurt. In that same time the Pentagon spent tens of millions of dollars and dropped tens of thousands of pounds of explosives on Vietnam, killing or wounding thousands of human beings, causing hundreds of millions of dollars of damage. Because nothing justified their actions in our calculus, nothing could contradict the merit of ours."

Jerry was welcomed into the Chicago tribe of the Weather Underground with open arms. His military experience and training were bound to come in handy. When the group was running through training exercises in Lincoln Park yelling KILL THE PIGS, KILL THE PIGS, Jerry remembered bayonet training at Fort Gordon where the racist and obscene KILL THE GOOK, KILL THE GOOK expletive was yelled as he charged into the dummy target. He decided on his own chant for Chicago--KILL THE WAR, KILL THE WAR, KILL THE WAR!

I didn't give up on the peace candidacy of Senator Eugene McCarthy of Minnesota even though the police had tried to discourage me with their batons and Mace. I took the big red Plymouth out to Omaha, Nebraska where the McCarthy campaign assigned me to a precinct in a black neighborhood. At one two flat I walked upstairs to the apartment of Johnny Smith. He wasn't there but his white girlfriend was friendly and kept me talking for quite a while. Her luscious full pale white tits were 90 percent on display and a serious challenge to my integrity. I finally broke down and asked about some treats, but she said, "Sorry, too late now, Johnny's due home any minute."

I pressed on but was somewhat discouraged by the number of homes that sported framed pictures of John F. Kennedy. One even had a candle burning under it.

At about 11:00 that evening a friend from Chicago and I left the bar in the Kennedy headquarters hotel in downtown Omaha where we had enjoyed some beers. Robert Kennedy's limo pulled up as we were standing there on the sidewalk in front of the hotel. He noticed our Eugene buttons and stopped to talk. He wondered why we were supporting McCarthy. I told him that I knew his brother had a lot to do with starting the war and since he had worked with his brother, I assumed he was guilty as well. He defended his current antiwar position. I asked about his support for the dirty wars against liberation movements in Latin America. He was incredibly open and persuasive. Another five minutes and I probably would have changed sides.

CHAPTER 38

California

The next stop on the campaign trail was the biggest prize of all, California, where the clean for Gene, Eugene McCarthy crowd was strong in affluent suburbs and around all the college and university communities. Bobby's strength was with the Latinos who followed the lead of Cesar Chavez and went for him in a big way. The blacks loved him as well. The Asians were the next largest minority and they too were solidly for Kennedy.

The weekend before the big primary I was in Detroit for some drug sales training compliments of Parke Davis. A nurse from Toronto who had treated me well in Acapulco drove over for a visit. Unfortunately, the training was rigorous and two local women had kept me up late the night before, so I was worthless to her. My flight back to Chicago was only half full. I had noticed that the flight was going on to Los Angeles, so I carried on my bag and slept through the stop in Chicago and got a free ride to L.A.

A young woman on the flight who was on her way to Hawaii for a short vacation latched on to me as I lingered at her seat admiring her blouse on my way to the washroom. She was determined to enjoy her vacation, so we rented a room near the airport for some amorous exercise. We had warmed up nicely on the long flight into strong headwinds and continued to devour each other in the taxi. Clothes went flying as we entered the sparse room. She tried to get my dick just where she wanted it but remembering my bookstore education, I was determined to get this one right.

"Kiss my inner thigh," she seemed to beg.

"Like this?" I asked as I wrapped my lips around as fine a piece of lady flesh as you could imagine. I put my right hand under her left knee and my left hand under her firm white ass. I worked on that gem like it was a piece of watermelon. I tongued from knee to the blonde forest and back to the knee. The sun shone through the top of the shade and revealed pale white, creamy, alabaster skin begging for more. With Willy under control I tarried at heaven's gate then dove in as she moaned, "More, more, more." I didn't ask more "what" but when she pulled my face into her and started bouncing, I got the picture.

I got her in a cab back to the airport in time for her connection then went right back to the room and had a much-needed nap. I went to the McCarthy office for an assignment and spent an hour telling Rob Reiner about the war. The Vietnam Veterans Against the War had a table in the office. I considered signing on with the VVAW but remember telling a guy that I was afraid to get my name on their list even though I agreed with them totally.

Election day, June 5,1968, arrived on schedule. I worked my assigned precinct and headed to the McCarthy headquarters hotel to enjoy the victory party. If each county had counted equally, McCarthy would have won handily with thirty-eight compared to Kennedy's mere eighteen. However, Kennedy carried all the heavily populated California counties including Los Angeles and ended up with about 100,000 more votes total. It was close but McCarthy was out.

While I was crying in my beer that night at the "victory" party, Robert Kennedy was assassinated at the nearby Beverly Hilton Hotel. I naively thought the killing would put my candidate back in the race. Kennedy had locked up all the California delegates and they went to Chicago determined to vote the party line. In the primaries 82 percent of the vote went to peace candidates. Humphrey did not run in a single primary, but he was the chosen candidate of the Democratic party that August in the Chicago war zone. Chosen by the war machine mysteriously called democracy.

The Chicago Democratic convention was held in late August 1968. McCarthy's most celebrated delegate was the movie star Paul Newman. Since I had the big red Plymouth, I was assigned to be his driver, valet and gofer. While walking down Michigan Avenue near the Conrad Hilton hotel with Paul on August 28th, the police riot was in full swing. I flipped the bird at a cop walking towards me. He gave me a strange familiar look. I realized I knew him. He worked a beat near a Chicago Boys Club on the West side where I had worked as a social worker before going to the war. I had dealt with kids who had been kicked out of the club. Had Paul noticed my poor behavior he would have fired me on the spot.

The next morning, I was on duty bright and early and met Paul and Arthur Miller, a famous writer and an ex of Marilyn Monroe, for breakfast in the basement cafe at the Hilton. I had bacon and eggs while they munched on honeydew melon and blueberries. I signed for the bill as the McCarthy rep on duty but forgot to leave a tip. The waitress was doubly disappointed, and I still regret not leaving her a tip and something signed by Paul.

I drove Paul to and from the Convention Center and put up with whatever Hollywood riffraff wanted to ride along instead of waiting for the convention center bus. One of the riders was actor Jill St John and later I was asked to escort her to a McCarthy party at a local club. I declined and hurried home to the waiting arms of a very nervous Muy Ba who had been watching the melee on television. This riot was so serious that the eventual candidate, Hubert Humphrey, was slammed by tear gas while in the shower at the Hilton.

While all this was going on in the streets with the police battling 10,000 antiwar protestors, Senator Abraham Ribicoff was nominating the peace candidate Senator George McGovern and used his time at the podium to condemn the Gestapo tactics being used in the streets. Mayor Daley took exception to the harsh characterization of his thugs and yelled from the floor, "Fuck you, you Jew son of a bitch! You lousy motherfucker! Go home." At the same time the protesters in Grant Park were chanting "The whole world is watching; the whole world is watching." Imagine that!

My last convention duty was to drive Paul back to the airport. We had to stop at a drugstore on the way to pick up *The Chicago Sun Times*. He turned quickly to the movie reviews. *Rachel, Rachel* had just been released starring his wife, Joanne Woodward. Paul was the director. He seemed pleased with the review but soon slipped into a bit of melancholy. He had higher hopes for the Democratic Party. I told him I didn't think the rich should have servants. I was so fucking clueless!

At the airport his private pilot showed up in the American Airlines Admirals Club where I was waiting with Paul for his flight. The pilot needed cash and neither of them had any checks, so I offered a check and marked out my name. Paul filled it out for $50 and signed it. The pilot was pleased with the money and headed back to town. Unfortunately, the money was deducted from my meager account even though I had crossed out my name, so I had to explain to an incredulous banker what happened. I got my $50 back but lost a fine souvenir!

CHAPTER 39

La Pasionara

Bill Ayers and his various tribes from around the country had not been especially disappointed by the outcome of the convention because they hadn't expected the Democrats to nominate a candidate who was opposed to their own war. Plans proceeded on schedule to bring the war home with the "days of rage" as we referred to our upcoming action. Bill told me the plan was to rally with thousands of working-class kids from the base cities and the militants from our collectives at seven thirty in Lincoln Park on that first night of the Days of Rage, but it didn't work out like that. By eight, when Jerry and I slipped in from the north, no more than a couple hundred people were milling idly around a small fire I'd passed. I don't remember how many cops were stationed just out of sight, fully armed and poised to strike--we weren't only outnumbered and outgunned, we might just be out of our minds. My stomach sank. Where were all the revolutionary youth? I felt like running away, slipping into the darkness and disappearing, but I knew I couldn't or wouldn't. Our objective was to make it all the way downtown, to assault the Federal Building full force, with a tough and multiplying youth army, to smash the windows and batter the walls, to once more enact our outrage and rehearse our resistance. There's no turning back now, I knew, and tried to remember the Granma, the launch that took Fidel Castro and Che to Cuba from Mexico where they were promptly jailed.

This, then, was the hardcore stripped bare, the collective members from Michigan, Ohio, Colorado, Maryland. But it slowly became, for all its deflated weirdness, an exciting sight for me---a small, determined group suited up for battle, everyone wearing an odd motorcycle or army-surplus helmet, many with goggles and gas masks, heavy boots and gloves, pants and shirts taped securely at ankles and wrists. Some looked like warriors, some more like clowns. David appeared to be going out to collect Halloween candy in oversized orange coveralls, motorcycle boots, and a World War I helmet several sizes too small perched on his bespeckled egg-shaped head. Terry looked like a rogue Cub Scout bent on mischief. Jerry looked like he had just gotten out of the Army and flown in from the Haight Ashbury neighborhood of San Francisco. Well, of course, he had. He wore his Army jungle boots and fatigues with exaggerated bell bottoms for a fine bohemian look. The front of his fatigues was tie-dyed with rainbow colors for a pure hippie-soldier look. Jerry felt that he was a hippie-soldier going to war against war. "War against war," he said to himself again and seemed to like the sound of it.

Stashed out of sight and in backpacks and under jackets, most of us carried an arsenal of unanticipated street weapons: steel pipes and slingshots, chains, clubs, mace, and rolls of pennies to add weight to a punch. No one had a gun, but no one would be helplessly assaulted tonight either, I thought. Bill said we would up the stakes again, and again we'd pay the price. How high? High, Bill guessed, but had no real idea as he waded into the group and we greeted one another with desperate hugs. Bill found Diana quickly, and soon the entire affinity group was fully assembled---Terry, Diana, Rachel, Ruthie, David, Fiona, and Bill. They would fight side by side, protect one another from harm, and try their best to break every window in their righteous path.

Before long, our bonfire was full up, feeding on large pieces of splintered park benches we'd randomly smashed up for fuel. The cool air crackled, the mist receded some, and then the crowd roared and I remember looking west to see a contingent of chanting fighters break fiercely through the fog and wheel into the park--maybe a hundred or a hundred and fifty strong, but maybe, just maybe, in their determination, a thousand or even ten thousand. "Ho, Ho, Ho Chi Minh, the Viet Cong Are Gonna Win." What a sight--this lovely little guerilla army in tight, disciplined formation, two abreast, approaching and then surrounding the bonfire quickly, purposefully, and pivoting smartly to face the rest of us, leading chants punctuated with war whoops and ear-piercing whistles. The collective energy surged; the tension turned thick.

Bill said at this point his blood became hot, his forehead ice cold, sparks leaping from his skin. He was not kidding--I looked at the backs of his hands and little blue and white electric currents danced wildly across them. When he turned to show Diana, holding his hands aloft, she glanced past them and stared instead at his face. "What happened?" she asked, sounding mystified. "How the hell did that happen?"

"What?"

"'Look at your glasses."

He pulled them off and sure enough, each lens was a little starburst of tiny cracks and fissures spidering out from the center. He hadn't been hit or bumped, hadn't felt a thing beyond the weird electric light show--but his glasses were shattered. "Shit," he said, puzzled, but also a little delighted then dazzled. This was so, so strange. The chanting escalated, sending sparks into the night sky, and the theater of revolution filled the park. We shouted and buoyed each other up, clinging to the lifeboat of our hope and each other. Terry circled away to greet late-arriving comrades, and I held tight standing with Bill and Jerry.

Somewhere we knew that a killer wave was gathering in the gloom beyond, and secretly hoped someone would show up on a rescue ship and pull us all to safety. But it seemed doubtful, impossible. And soon we didn't care.

The feverish revelry was at a peak when Bernardine Dohrn appeared on a slight rise to the left of the fire and the troops exploded into a chanting frenzy. "Ho, Ho, Ho, Ho Chi Minh, the NLF is Gonna Win!" She was wearing a black leather jacket over a black turtleneck, her trademark short skirt and high stylish black boots, an eyeliner pencil peeking from her breast pocket. Her blazing eyes were allied with elegance. She had earned her role as the voice and the leader of the militants through practice, but she was also a stunning and seductive symbol of the Revolutionary Woman--J. Edgar

Hoover had dubbed her "La Pasionara of the lunatic left"---and as she stood in that frenzied park late that night, her dark hair whipped by the wind, her brilliant eyes flashing in answer to the fire, we would have followed her anywhere.

She raised one hand and the park was suddenly, eerily quiet: "Brothers and sisters," she shouted into the emptiness. "It's time for mother country radicals to take our place in a worldwide struggle. It's time to BRING THE WAR HOME!"

A roar erupted, and the chanting began anew. She could write legal briefs or law review articles, handle a crowd, or brave a police assault. She could concoct fantastic plans, and she was a captivating speaker. "Tonight, is the anniversary of Che's murder," she said. "But Che's death has not killed the revolution." Cheers and whistles filled the air. Che lives! *Venceremos*! Ho, Ho, Ho, Chi Minh! The refrain reverberated through the park, echoing, beguiling, and finally hypnotic.

When the chanting slowed, Tom Hayden, on trial in federal court with seven others on conspiracy charges for leading the demonstrations at the Democratic Convention a year earlier, emerged from the crowd. When his trial had begun in late September a group of us had disrupted the proceedings, and now Hayden was bearing an echo of solidarity to us: "I bring greetings from the Chicago Eight," he said. "We love you! We are with you!"

"Ho, Ho, Ho Chi Minh," we sang in answer, and Hayden added, "Anything that intensifies our resistance to this war is in the service of humanity. The Weathermen are setting the terms for all of us now. Tear this monster down!" Tom was caught up in the spirit of the moment and shedding the careful demeanor he had practiced in court, became the old inciter. Our chants escalated again and swirled like fireworks into the air. As improbable as it all was, I felt giddy and newly emboldened. We were about to leap arm-in-arm into the inferno of the unknown, and I remember trembling with giddiness and holding on to Bill and Diana.

The night was darker and deeper, the air colder, when Jeffrey Jones, heavily costumed with wig and helmet and paste-on beard but easily recognizable to the comrades, leapt to the front and, evoking our little monster icon, the ten-year-old boy who had derailed a train that year in Italy with a chunk of concrete, shouted, "I am Marion Delgado!" A great roar engulfed him. "We're heading down to derail the train of injustice! Tonight, this city is ours!"

A little path opened, and Jones began to head south in a hard run, and three comrades linked arms in neat synchronization to his left, three to his right. We fell into quick formation behind, lines of eight to twelve people materializing like magic out of the mist. My group was intact, front row. Hundreds of us left the park that way, at a sprint, without any resistance at all--the cops had prepared for last year's battle, huddled to the north ready to contain us when we defied the curfew, but instead we stormed south into the city, into the world beyond, rocking them back on their heels. We were in full attack.

We shrieked and screamed as we ran, undulating in imitation of the fighters of *The Battle of Algiers*. I saw us become what I thought was a real battalion in a guerrilla army, and it felt for that moment more than theater, more than metaphor. I felt the warrior rising up inside me--- audacity and courage, righteousness, of course, and more audacity.

As we plunged out of the park on to North Avenue and Clark Street, David and Rachel hauled chunks of brick and pavement from pockets and packs and hurled a barrage at the huge inviting windows of the first building on the block, a big and gleaming bank. The glass shattered and a vibration exploded through us. It was Pavlov's bell. As in the collectives months ago, the competition was on, each act inspiring another. The bigger the mess the better was the incentive zinging in my brain. The crowd thundered down Clark, every windowpane a target, every bit of glass in every business crashing joyously in our wake, hotel windows, the windows of the luxury high-rise apartments we streamed past. I swung my Billy club into the windshield of a Cadillac and then a Mercedes.

The streets became sparkling and treacherous with the jagged remains of our rampage, and we had to dance lightly in our heavy boots to avoid diving into the crystal chaos. I kept watching for a comrade to go down, knowing the result would be something like death by a thousand cuts, but no one did. On we charged, slip-sliding away.

We heard sirens now, but saw no barricades, no massed police presence, and we were moving fast. Suddenly a single cop car appeared half a block ahead, lights flashing, and someone yelled authoritatively, "Stay in formation! Stay in formation!" I don't think it was me; maybe it was David. We swarmed over and around that car, smashing windows, slashing tires, trashing lights and fenders---it seemed the only conceivable thing to do. I leapt from the trunk to the roof to the cheers of friends, jumped up and down several times until it caved in slightly, and then slid off easily and kept moving, glancing back to see a broken shell with two cops hunkered down in the front seat, one's eyes opened and starring in vacant disbelief, the other's locked on me with what felt like murderous intention. In a second, I was beyond reach.

Then a real barricade materialized just ahead, serious with several cars and hundreds of cops. Several affinity groups split on to side streets and kept moving. We veered east two blocks, and then south again, smashing everything in reach. Another barricade, another sharp turn and a rapid readjustment, on and on, stampeding through the night on the Gold Coast toward the heart of the city.

At this point Jerry noticed a mounted cop leading his horse toward an old black woman I hadn't noticed before. She was holding a sign that read "War Takes Lives, Peace Takes Brains." She was obviously about to die for peace or get seriously injured. Jerry had grown up with horses and took command of the situation. He grabbed the horse's bridle and stopped it instantly. The angry cop tried to whack Jerry with his baton, but Jerry moved the horse's head so that the cop hit his own horse in the head. The cop tried the other side with the same result. That was enough for the horse. He sat down suddenly throwing the idiot pig off backwards. Jerry quickly removed the horse's tack for its safety and it decided to run free with the Weathermen, the first obvious convert of the evening!

Down on Monroe Street just east of the loop Bill noticed that a fat cop who had been trying to catch them had sat down to catch his breath. Bill and Jerry and I decided to smash the doors of the two-story Brooks Brothers men's clothing store nearby. The cop sauntered over and into the store. He knew what he was doing and went straight to the double ply cashmere sweaters on the second floor. At $398 a pop, the armload he left with would cover another trip to his favorite hooker in Las Vegas which is where he really wanted to be.

Unfortunately for him the security cameras caught him, and he made the front page of the *Chicago Tribune* along with a caption that read "Days of Rage a Bonanza for Cops." I recognized him. A few months earlier I saw a guy breaking into a fancy car loaded with luggage on Michigan Avenue and ran to him since he was the nearest cop. He had struggled just to walk the two blocks. The thief and the suitcases were long gone when we got there. I left him with the sad tourists and saw that he was talking on his radio, his usual air of authority slowly returning.

Jerry, Bill and I continued west buoyed by the thought of our hapless pursuer being so easily sidetracked. Soon the flashing lights and whining alarms were all in the distance, echoing only in our heads, but we sped on until we were completely swallowed by the huge and buoyant night. With no one chasing us now we sat down on a bench in front of Zimmerman's Liquor. Jerry said, "Bill I gotta tell you this is the best I have felt about the war since I first arrived in Vietnam."

"Why is that?" Bill wondered.

"Just watching the lies on the news everyday makes me sick. I see feeble attempts at protest just plain ignored or belittled by the pols. Now I am literally elated because I just know what we are doing tonight here in Chicago will get their attention."

"Something better get their attention soon," Bill said as his breathing slowed a little. He looked at the liquor store window and saw an ad for Coors beer which was just showing up from Colorado. "A real beer would sure go down nicely about now but I tried that watery Coors piss once out in Denver. Never again."

"I prefer a good union made beer like Budweiser," Jerry offered as they got up and continued heading west.

Eventually Bill and Jerry stopped again. Bill looked up and was completely disoriented, lost in a maze of warehouses and loading docks, cracked and crumbling concrete, deserted streets. Bill thought, where was I? Behind them the city was ablaze, the country choking on evil. He knew Chicago up and down, inside and out, but he'd never seen this before. They were somewhere west of the Loop, and still a little north. They wandered around for a while with Bill hoping to get his bearings. He never did. They could smell the river, heaven was brilliant, the moon glowing in the cold still air, the stars trembling in the wide sky. Where was Diana? Bill made a little wish then, a wish for survival. A wish that he'd inherited from his mom for all occasions; He wished that everything would turn out fine.

Just then they were startled as a phantom hurried past mumbling, more shade than human, but a flesh and blood human man, nonetheless. He appeared out of nowhere, a watch cap pulled down over his ears, an oversized filthy trench coat flapping around his scrawny frame. "Yo baby, yo baby, yo baby," he muttered over and over, glancing at us vaguely. "C'mon, man, let's go. C'mon man." He never shut up, and for some reason we fell mindlessly in step with him. We didn't have a better idea. We cruised together down the block into an alley that opened onto a dirt path leading through some scrubby brush near the river. The path ended at a broken iron staircase, and we followed Mumbles as he plunged underground, his heavy unlaced boots rebounding noisily on each step. "C'mon man, C'mon."

At the bottom we climbed over and around a graveyard of wrecked and abandoned cars, skirted a well-lit section of road, and plunged finally into a chaos of heavy cardboard packing crates and lean-tos. Once inside, the tangled outlines of this fugitive city became plain, rows of improvised shelters, haphazard sleeping quarters, piles of mattresses and old clothes here and there, little campfires dotting the landscape, each the center of a huddle of John Steinbeck hobos or---and recently homeless Vietnam veterans. Mumbles led us deep into this strange city and parked us at a large fire with maybe a dozen ragged spirits basking in the warmth. Yo, Brother Red, Mumbles called to an imposing man with a small felt fedora cocked atop his large head with a heavy woolen blanket tossed around his shoulders. Look here, Brother Red, I found us two more.

Brother Red laughed warmly and stepped out to greet us with wonderful bear hugs. We, felt tiny and white and suddenly totally exhausted in his presence with the stench of tear gas clinging to our bloody clothes as the warmth of the fire pulled us in. He paused for a moment looking us over then asked if we were with them? Bill asked with who?

One of them revolutionary brothers, he said. One of them--what do you call em?--Weathermen. We confessed that we sure as hell were. Brother Red pulled crates up to the fire for us and made introductions all around.

Brother Red was a large block of a man with an open reddish face and round, watery eyes. He had a halo of long frizzy gray hair, the circle made complete by an exploding full beard. He was a storyteller and a critic, and he loved to talk. Yes friends, those Chicago cops getting what they deserve, just chickens coming home to roost.

They haven't had the time to come and roust us for a few days now, and for that alone I salute you gentle weathermen. He laughed at his way with words. The brothers passed around fine tasting cheap maybe double cheap wine which now tasted better than the finest French estate bottled wine. We had several candy bars which we shared. What does he mean, another one? Bill asked.

Brother Red enjoyed another laugh and explained that this jungle is about the end of the line---it's the lost and the lonely here, folks that's on the loose and on the run. Yep, we get them all, outcasts and outlaws, irregulars and illegitimates, and tonight two of your brothers-in-arms beat you here by half an hour---oh, and both of those brothers are actually sisters.

Mumbles led us down the line to a packing crate, and pushed a cloth aside, ducked and entered. Inside Diana bent over a bloody young woman stretched out sleeping on an old mattress. "Oh my God," Bill said. Diana looked up, her face tight, exhausted and strained, but without a hint of surprise to see us there.

When Bill kissed her face, he could see a large lump on the side of her head, and he could see she had been crying. She told us that she'd been with the group on Lake Shore Drive when the melee there broke out. She'd fought in close formation with several others, and as the fighters retreated slowly toward a construction site locked in combat, the cops had suddenly disengaged and vanished. In a flash a shotgun blast cut through their midst. Most broke and ran, but at least three went down, a guy from the New York collective and this one bleeding on the mattress. Incredibly they had escaped arrest.

"She's a local high school kid," Diana said. "She's got buckshot in her left side. She's going to be OK, but what a mess."

We talked through the night. Brother Red looked in on us twice, once bringing water and once word that the radio was reporting that twenty-eight cops had been injured and one hundred comrades had been locked up. He could hardly contain his glee, and what looked like pride in his watery eyes." Twenty-Eight," he repeated with a chuckle. "God-damn."

The school kid slept only fitfully and asked for water several times. After Jerry gave her some water in a plastic cup, she put her head back down on her pillow which was someone's down vest wrapped in a piece of sheeting. He comforted her with a pat on her sweet young head and told her, while fighting back tears, that she reminded him of his wife Sally.

CHAPTER 40

Ho Ho Ho ... Ho Chi Minh

Sally and Muy Ba stayed up all night at the house on Seminary. Muy Ba was especially buoyant at one point during the live TV coverage, and Sally asked her why.

"When our friends sing Ho, Ho, Ho... Ho Chi Minh the NLF is gonna win, I just know it's true and I'm so glad our friends are really bring the war home to America. They just break some windows to remind people there is a war going on. They don't hurt nobodys."

"What about the twenty-eight injured cops we heard about?" Sally asked.

"Oh, they just fall off their horses and get cut while stealing from the fancy stores. I heard on the radio that a cop went into Peacock's Jewelry Store and was so mad that all the good jewelry was locked in the safe that he hit the safe with his fist and had to go to the hospital with a broken hand. I don't understand why you call them pigs. Vietnamese pigs are much smarter than your Chicago cops."

Sally quickly corrected Muy Ba, "Don't forget I'm from San Francisco, so they are not my pigs, and I'm not sure it is a good idea to be cheering for the Communist leader Ho Chi Minh."

Muy Ba then realized that just because someone like Sally was against the war did not mean she supported the communists. She said, "All my life the communists in Vietnam have been fighting to end white colonialism. My father proudly promoted agrarian reform in the south when all of Vietnam was united after World War II."

"What does that have to do with Ho Chi Minh?"

"He returned from exile in France when he was fifty-five years old to help us fight for our independence. Yes, he had started the Communist Party of Vietnam in Paris but in his heart, he was first of all a nationalist."

"Well I sure hope the war ends," Sally said, "but I still think communists are godless and bad and I don't like it when our friends sing about Ho Chi Minh."

"Would you rather hear them sing "Nix, Nix, Nix, time to Nix Nixon peace is gonna win?"

"Actually yes, that sounds pretty good."

Meanwhile back in the trenches under Wacker Drive with the bright blue sky delivered compliments of Lake Michigan, the gang said their goodbyes to their wonderful new friends, Big Red and Mumbles. Peaches, the horse, was munching contentedly on a patch of weedy grass by the river as they kissed him and thanked him for his outstanding service to the cause of peace. Antiwar work brings out the best in a lot of people and obviously critters too.

CHAPTER 41

Fred Hampton

The work I had been doing with the Chicago Black Panther Party came to a sad and tragic end with the assassination of Chairman Fred Hampton on December 4th, 1969. The actual murder was carried out by Chicago police in blue, but they were mere puppets directed by J. Edgar Hoover's FBI. FBI agents were in on the raid but let the local cops do the shooting. The Citizens Commission to Investigate the FBI obtained records in March of 1971 which exposed the super-secret and illegal COINTELPRO program. Its goal was the disruption of activities of the black liberation movement. The killings of Malcolm X and Martin Luther King, Jr., were masked so that the direct connection to the federal government was not clearly established. If Muhammed Ali and Doctor King had not come out forcefully against the war in Vietnam, this war against black leaders may not have materialized.

Fred Hampton was a brilliant and beautiful 21-year-old black man who had the speaking ability and charisma to move the people towards liberation. Direct action was our government's answer to the threat he posed. A few days before the assassination I attended a rally in downtown Chicago where he said, "You can kill a revolutionary, but you can't kill a revolution."

CHAPTER 42

Paris

A letter finally came directly to Muy Ba from her father. It was postmarked Paris, France. Muy Ba and I returned home from a visit to Sally and Jerry's place on Montana Street to find Stokes Riley, our mail carrier, sitting on the bench on our front porch waving the precious letter like a fan. Stokes had a big smile on his handsome face because he knew Muy Ba was hoping her parents would write once they got to Paris for the long-awaited peace talks. As she reached for it, he pulled it back and made her say, "Please." Stokes walked down the stairs saying, "I hope it's good news for you two." We went inside with the letter and sat together on the loveseat in the living room to read it.

It was exactly what they were hoping for. The peace talks were finally starting, and Muy Ba's mother Madame

Giap had tagged along with General Giap with high hopes of seeing her prodigal daughter.

Of course, Muy Ba and Larry flew to Paris on the next available flight. The economy seats were sold out but for some reason they were given first class seats at no extra charge. Since they were on Air France, Muy Ba said, *"Quel fantastique!"* as they settled in for a gourmet dinner with fine wine.

They were met at Paris Orly Airport by a car sent by the Vietnamese delegation to the peace talks. Their sightseeing trip to their hotel provided stunning views of the Arc de Triomphe and Notre Dame which Muy Ba said looked just like Notre Dame in Saigon. The River Seine boat tour on the *Bretagne* looked so exciting that they agreed to come back soon and take the tour that left from Notre Dame. The voice of the French national treasure Edith Piaf drifted in the air as they passed. Muy Ba said Piaf was a favorite of her father and Ho Chi Minh. She hoped that Edith would still be singing when they took their boat ride.

When their car pulled up at the Hotel Mercure Paris Montparnasse Raspail, they were both sure it had to be the wrong place. It looked expensive but was actually inexpensive for the neighborhood, near the Luxembourg Gardens. When they got to their room there were flowers for Muy Ba from her parents. The card was signed by her mother. Muy Ba was thrilled to be so close after all the months since their last visit at the wedding in Ben Luc. A note inside from Mom said that she should call Room 319 so we could make plans to go to dinner.

Muy Ba called right away and asked to meet immediately. Her mom said, "Please come now but come by yourself so your wonderful Larry won't see me crying."

When Muy Ba came back to our room she said that they mostly just hugged and cried. They were so happy they didn't seem to know what to say. But there was a plan for dinner at Le Roquet It was nearby at the corner of Rue des Saints-Peres and Boulevard Saint Germain in the Left Bank neighbor-hood. With formica tables and deep red vinyl booths, it didn't look like a proper meeting place for the most important diplomat in town but soon enough General Giap and Madame came smiling through the front door. I was so happy to see them that I ran to greet them and walked them to our booth.

The General was in a good mood because it seemed that the peace talks were going well. The grouchy looking waiter perked up when the General, speaking perfect French, ordered a bottle of Chateau Latour, Medoc, France, 1950. Ho Chi Minh had raved about it and wanted to know if it was still as good as he remembered. At $4,370 a bottle it was probably still quite good but we all laughed and settled for the waiters recommendation for a more recent and considerably less dear vintage.

Then things got serious when the General asked how the antiwar movement was proceeding in the states. I said, "We have been working with the Black Panther Party and the Weathermen. The Black Panthers definitely have the most potential for shutting down the war."

Doctor King denounced the war in an incredible speech at Riverside Church in New York City on April 4, 1967, where he acknowledged his respect for the organizers of the group, Clergy and Laymen Concerned about Vietnam. He pledged his support for their statement, "A time comes when silence is betrayal."

"In Vietnam," King said, "That time has come for us."

Because of the volcanic impact of Doctor King's words and the potential for others such as the eloquent and charismatic Fred Hampton to replace the murdered King, the U.S. government went on a killing spree to silence black antiwar leaders.

The Weathermen were not only white, they were upper middle class and even rich. J. Edgar Hoover treated them with kid gloves because he was too ignorant to see that they also represented a major threat to the pro war coalition in power in Washington.

I told about the days of rage and our friend Jerry's chant, "Kill the War, Kill the War." The General almost fell over backwards in his chair laughing about Jerry's encounter with the mounted cop who hit his own horse in the head until it sat down throwing him off.

After the wonderful casual French dinner, the General and Madame went back to the hotel and Muy Ba said, "Now Larry Ryan, you will walk me to the gardens that we saw on the way to the hotel."

I said, "Great idea" and started walking east.

"No, no, no, silly," Muy Ba said, "They are back this way."

Of course, she was right again. We shortly saw an old black and white sign with an arrow pointing west that said Tuileries Garden in English and French. We walked hand in hand down Alee Centrale for a few minutes and were soon at the east entrance, 113 Rue de Rivioli, looking up at the sculptures called the "Winged Horses" in the oldest park in gay Paree. The sign said the horses were just copies and the originals were in the Louvre. I wondered if this is what the American soldiers were talking about during World War I when they sang "How will you keep them down on the farm after they've seen *gay Paree*?"

Muy Ba didn't miss a beat, "Let's go to the Louvre to see them! I want you to see that sweet girl Mona Sue anyway."

"Do you by any chance mean the *Mona Lisa* by Michelangelo?"

"Yes, Larry, you are so smart except in Hanoi they said the artist's name was Leonardo da Vinci."

Wow I finally outsmarted her. Or did I? We'll find out it was Michelangelo when we see it, I'm sure. Then I tried to take her picture, but she pointed her finger at me and said, "No, no, no, silly." She took my hand and led me past a row of amazing sculptures of mythological figures, all nude and lovely. We walked on south to the Musee de L'Orangerie where we admired Monet's "Les Nympheas" which reminded Muy Ba of the park by her house in Hanoi. "I wonder if Monet visited Hanoi, these water lilies look just like ours," she said. I smiled. Monet bought a house in Giverny in 1890. The house came with a pond full of water lilies which of course he painted. In the middle of the garden we came to two cafes separated by a wide gravel path. "The gravel is nice," she said. "It lets the rain go down instead of running to the lake with all the dirt like it does in Chicago. We are lucky the French supervised the building of our parks instead of the Americans."

The cafes both had snacks and coffee so we sat down on comfortable tea chairs with tables attached for pastry and cafe au lait. "This is so nice," Muy Ba said. "I feel guilty though about enjoying myself since the war is still tearing apart our friends and their families back in Cu Chi." Letting go of her guilt Muy Ba said, "My father wants us to visit the cemetery *Pere la Chaise*. He has memorized the words of many French people and wonders if these famous French people are buried there.

He most often quotes Napoleon Bonaparte who said, "Religion is What Keeps the Poor from Murdering the Rich." He also likes Denis Diderot who said more than one hundred years ago, "Man will never be free until the last king is strangled with the entrails of the last priest."

"That can't be what your father thinks. Have you forgotten about your Irish priest back in Guam?"

"Well of course the Irish are different!"

I was relieved and said, "OK, then let's go."

In the morning there was a knock on the door but no one was there. I looked down on the floor and saw a lovely tray with coffee and croissants and a newspaper. I brought the tray into the room and Muy Ba almost screamed, "The French people love us too, Larry! How can we be at war with so many nice people?"

I said, "If they really loved us don't you think *Le Figaro* would be in English for me?"

"Oh, Larry you sound like such an Ugly American. I will read it for you if you'll put butter and strawberry jam on a croissant for me. And pour some coffee with the hot milk. I just love *cafe au lait!*"

"Oh, shut up," I said with a smile as she started to translate an article about the war in Vietnam for me.

The phone rang and Muy Ba answered it and immediately started talking to her mother about all the great French people who were not buried in Pere la Chaise. I soon learned that the General would be busy most of the day and Madame would be sightseeing with us. We got directions to the Metro and took it to a stop conveniently named *Pere la Chaise*. We walked upstairs and were at the main entrance to the cemetery.

"Let's go see Edith," Muy Ba said as she pulled me to the map. So in seconds we were looking at several tombs in the Piaf section with the biggest belonging to

Edith. It was adorned with Christ on the cross and fresh cut flowers. France will never forget her.

"OK, my turn," I said. "Take me to Oscar Wilde, *sil vous plait.*"

"*Tres bon*," she said, obviously pleased with my French. She took us straight to Oscar. "What's so special about him?" she asked.

"Well he was a genius and he wrote many books and plays and said many witty things."

"Name one," she said.

"Sure he was probably thinking of you anyway when he said, 'Crying is for plain women. Pretty women go shopping.'" Madame cringed at that, but I had one more.

"Always forgive your enemies; nothing annoys them so much." Madame smiled at that one and to put an end to the cemetery visit. I said, "OK that's enough cemetery viewing, let's go to lunch."

Not being one to give up easily, Muy Ba said, "Victor Hugo is just around the next corner."

I remembered Victor Hugo from the Ao Dai Temple in Tay Ninh where I saw his portrait hanging like a saint at the front behind the altar. Well he was not just around the corner in this cemetery. He is buried at the Pantheon in Paris along with Emile Zola and Alexandre Dumas. We decided to save the great writer of *Les Miserables* and *The Hunchback of Notre Dame* for another day.

When we got back to the hotel we learned that the General had been called back to Hanoi for a meeting of the Politburo. Madame Giap was going with him. We were shocked and selfish. We didn't want this wonderful interlude to end. We rode along to the airport and this time I watched as Muy Ba and her Mom said their goodbyes, complete with a full complement of tears, Oscar Wilde be damned! General Giap shook my hand

and told me to go back to Chicago and continue the important task of bringing the war home. I told him we would be going to Washington to protest with the Vietnam Vets against the War. He hugged me, called me son and walked to his gate.

That evening we went back to Le Roquet by mistake. We were given the same table as the night before and Muy Ba just thought about her Mom having been right there and fought back tears. I ordered fish for her anyway and steak *pom frites* for myself. I had a glass of the same red wine and got her a glass of white Bordeaux. I had to drink both glasses. Hers was darn good too.

The next morning croissants and coffee came to the door again as the sun peeked over the Eiffel Tower. Muy Ba woke up smiling and was soon looking at a city guide and plotting our route to the Louvre.

We walked and walked back through the Luxembourg Gardens, past Notre Dame where we crossed the Seine to the Right Bank where we found the Louvre in all its splendor announcing our arrival in the 1st *arrondissement*. I wondered out loud why they didn't just call it a neighborhood and Muy Ba had to bite her tongue to keep from calling me an Ugly American again. All signs seemed to point to the Mona Lisa, so I guessed we were not the only ones looking for her.

Muy Ba said, "Look, there are the horses with wings from the Tuileries."

Now it was my turn to say, "No silly, that's Cupid or Eros who has just landed by Psyche."

"Oh yes Larry, you are so smart. It says Cupid is the son of Venus, the Goddess of beauty. He has much nicer wings than the horses at the garden and look at all those arrows in his quiver." I was wondering how she knew all this as we walked away from the sign she had read.

"Look up those stairs Larry, there's a pretty marble lady with nice wings but no head!"

We walked to the stairs and read that she is known as the *Winged Victory of Samothrace*. The boat she stands in weighs thirty tons! She is made of Parian marble and was created in ancient Greece about 200 years before the modern era.

Muy Ba said, "I sure am sorry she lost her head. We have better museums in Hanoi because our statues has a heads!"

We wandered towards Mona Lisa and finally there was the crowd of about fifty people waiting to see her. We decided to wait and eventually got close enough to be captivated by her incredible faint smile. We also saw that this most amazing painting was done by Leonardo da Vinci in the 16th century. What made me think Michelangelo had done it? Oh well she was right again, and I was learning to be proud of her knowledge and intelligence.

As we were walking back towards the entrance and trying to decide where to have lunch, she said out of the blue, "The *Hermitage* in Leningrad has more pictures and is much grander."

"How do you know?"

"I went with my father when I was small. He was there with Communists from New York City and Paris. The man from Paris knew all about Monet and Picasso and he told us the Hermitage was bigger and better than the Louvre."

Why argue I thought. Anyway, I knew Picasso was a Communist so why shouldn't the Hermitage have more of his paintings?

There were a lot of cafes in the Louvre, but we went back to the Tuileries Gardens where the nice little cafes on either side of the gravel path were so welcoming. The sandwiches we had were simple, but they were the best I had eaten since 1967 in Saigon. The baguettes were sliced in half and slathered with fresh warm butter and brown mustard. The ham was sliced very thin and the cheese looked like Swiss to me but tasted more like heaven. As we walked back to the hotel, I noticed Muy Ba was fighting back tears again.

The artists plying their trade along the Seine were a treat to watch as they turned plain canvas into boats afloat, churches like Notre Dame and people, people, people, eating, drinking, smoking and always kissing, kissing, kissing.

We confirmed our flights on Air France and headed home the next afternoon. Since our plane was speeding west, the sun never seemed to set, and I reveled in the feeling that our honeymoon would never end.

Jerry and Sally picked us up at the airport and it was good to be back home.

CHAPTER 43

Detroit

Back on Seminary Avenue Muy Ba was her usual cheerful self again. I walked to the Post Office and picked up our mail and filled out the card to have regular delivery resume. We sat together on the front porch looking through the mail. I was thrilled to see a letter from Joe Duffy and wondered what he could be writing about. We hadn't seen Joe since he was our best man at the wedding back in Ben Luc.

"Listen to this," I said and read aloud, "'The Vietnam Veterans against the War, VVAW, is sponsoring an investigation into war crimes in Vietnam in Detroit, Michigan. I think we should go. What do you think? Let me know right away if we're going so I can make plane reservations.' Wow, this is just what we need to do to make the General happy, don't you think?"

"I'm not so sure, maybe it will get your name in the paper and cause trouble for Bill and Bernadine and Jerry. What if Doctor Le Chang doesn't approve?"

"We could give him back the $50,000."

"No, we couldn't, silly. Did you forgets about all the dollars we spent for plane tickets to Paris and dinners and wines?"

I was excited about it. I thought I would probably see Mike McCusker again. He was the guy who first told me about VVAW at the McCarthy office in California. It would sure be good to see Joe and hopefully his wife, Judy.

Muy Ba picked up the phone and called the good doctor. She hurried through the story including her concerns.

"What'd he say?" I wondered.

"He said, The VVAW is the most effective antiwar group working in America. Then he corrected himself and said they were almost as effective as the Weathermen."

"Why don't we ask Bill what he thinks?" I said.

Bill arrived at the house on Seminary at cocktail time without Bernadette who was visiting her family at a retreat at Lake Geneva, Wisconsin. Al Capone had stayed at the very same resort, so it had to be safe we all hoped. We talked about the upcoming war crimes trial in Detroit and Bill gave me his wholehearted support. He wondered what I would testify about and I said, "I'm thinking I'll just answer whatever questions they throw at me as best I can."

"Just don't make up anything or it'll surely come back and bite you in the ass."

The trial date arrived, and we fired up the big red Plymouth and, with a nod to Parke Davis for providing first class transportation, headed to the Howard Johnson Motel on the north side of Detroit. Our room was pleasant with two double beds. I called Joe's room right away and found out we were scheduled to testify in Part II of the hearings which would start in the morning.

Unfortunately, Judy couldn't make it but the three of us had a fine time catching up over beers, burgers and deep-fried oysters. Jane Fonda sat at a table near us. Dressed in jeans and a simple tee shirt and reveling in the moment she would soon sacrifice a lot by traveling to Hanoi to try to find a way to end the war. Most soldiers who had been in Vietnam still thought the U.S. was trying to do something good in Vietnam and despised her for her high-profile antiwar actions. To be with this gang of motley vets who were inspired by her commitment to the movement was obviously just what she needed for dinner.

To understand what the VVAW had in mind by naming the trial the Winter Soldier investigation you need to know that in his collection of articles called *The American Crisis*, Thomas Paine's most famous article was called *Common Sense*. In it he wrote:

"These are the times that try men's souls: The summer soldier and the sunshine patriot will, in this crisis, shrink from the service of his country; but he that stands by it now, deserves the love and thanks of man and woman."

If presidential candidate Nixon and Henry Kissinger hadn't sabotaged the Paris Peace talks in 1968, Joe and I would not have been in Detroit trying to end the war in our own way. Jane Fonda would not have made her courageous trip to Hanoi and 20,000 fewer U.S. troops would have died in the war. More than 100,000 Americans were wounded, and more than a million

Vietnamese were killed because of what Nixon and Kissinger did. NOTE: George Will wrote of this in September 2014 referring to declassified documents.

Instead of being sentenced to death for treason, Nixon was elected president TWICE. The second time was after he got caught for the break-in at the Democratic Party headquarters at the Watergate Hotel in Washington, D.C. The commercial media preferred the criminal Nixon to the antiwar McGovern. Once Nixon's second term got underway, and he started to do things the media didn't like, he was dumped and replaced by perhaps our best president ever, Gerald Ford. Under Ford the Vietnam war was ended and the Pentagon budget was slashed. Cutting the Pentagon budget was not what the media had in mind, so Ford was drummed out with false charges of ineptitude. Then the military man, Jimmy Carter, was elected, and the sacred Pentagon budget was restored in full.

The next morning, we all made our way to the ballroom which was set up for the trial. After a few minutes of sweet rolls and coffee, Mike McCusker was introduced by Larry Rottmann who chaired the panel on press censorship. Mike testified that as a Marine information specialist, he witnessed torture routinely:

Mike McCusker:

"My witnessing of the torture of prisoners was generally on the field level whenever any particular outfit, whether it be squad size, company size, or battalion size, swept into a village on a search and destroy mission and captured prisoners. Which means any Vietnamese hanging around the village, or any Vietnamese flushed out of the bush, if he wasn't shot first. And they had field torture techniques: determining

who was going to go into the more refined tortures which involved somewhat the same type. In the field, it was the use of dogs after tying a suspect, who was any particular villager, to a tree and let the dog start yapping at his face, snapping at him. Field phones were wired to genitals, to nose, to ears. Threatenings were done with the knife, dunking in wells, dunking in rivers and streams. And we could write of none of these and if you did write of these they would be redlined. We could not write of recon fire missions. As I said before I was reconnaissance qualified and jump qualified. So I was the only man in recon trusted to go out with them--the only reporter-photographer the recon trusted because I knew their business. And recon was a little bit different than what I had been trained to do. Generally, in Vietnam you would take a few helicopters, land in an area, move out on top of a hill and call in arty strikes or air strikes in a particular given area. One particular time I watched a herd of elephants get hit by arty along with several villagers. I could never write about this. Could never write of how it was done and what the rationale for it was."

Mike goes on to explain what happened when he wrote the truth about the fighting. He said that if he wrote something that did not conform to the Marine's idea of what the news should be, it would be changed by a lifer who knew how to play the game.

Moderator:
"Next will be Larry Ryan who was with the 25th Infantry Division's 1st Brigade as a Brigade level information specialist. Now in the Army, the information specialists begin at battalion level. There

is supposed to be a brigade information specialist-- that's an enlisted man who collects the news; an information officer for each brigade. Larry, do you want to tell us a little about your experiences?"

Larry Ryan:

"Yes, I was in Cu Chi, Vietnam, during 1966 and 1967 and I've worked as a Public Information Office specialist. And, generally, I think what I have to talk about is what I perceived my job to be there and what it actually turned out to be. It was an overall cover up of what was actually going on in the division operation. During the time I was there with the 25th Division every news release that came out of our information office--that was at Brigade level and at Headquarters level with the division--made it appear that we were really winning the war; that we were doing a fantastic job.

"So, while people like Dave with the ¾ Cavalry were out getting their tracks blown off by one or two Viet Cong, we would write stories about these glorious victories that didn't take place. And generally, what I saw were how the figures were turned around on body counts. One particular time I was with the 3/4 Cavalry when three of our men got killed.

"Our men killed one young Vietnamese boy who was actually a prisoner at the time he was killed, laying in the grass in front of us. We counted graves that day in an old cemetery so the story that came out of our office was seventeen Viet Cong killed. What actually happened was that two or three Vietnamese had killed three of our men and if there had been a large force there, they left.

"But, overall, this is what my job was: to go out on these missions where nothing happened except that we might kill a few civilians, if we found them, and pretend that we were really winning some battles when, actually, it was Americans being killed."

Moderator:

"Larry, you mentioned you had trouble sort of perceiving what your job was at first. Did you ever write what you consider to be a truly objective news story? In other words, one based on the facts."

Larry Ryan:

"To me there was never any question about anyone wanting me to write about what I saw in the field. The job of our newspaper was to build morale in the field, and as a public information office, our job was to propagandize the American people. And this is what we would do. We would write propaganda, and at times I would go to the field and write a story that was personally related to what we saw taking place, but what was actually happening was that our people were being killed as they alienated the Vietnamese people in the villages that we went through on search and destroy missions. That was never what we would write about.

"One particular mission near Dau Tieng we lost about five men that day, but we happened to find some rice. Well, this was a big cache. Fine. So, we made it into a real victory. We didn't see the Vietnamese Communists who shot at us. They left. They killed several of our men and left. We found some rice. Well, the story that I wrote, which is the kind of job that I had, was that we had a very successful mission. I didn't

mention that the rice was marked, Houston, Texas. This was not allowed. Any of the rice caches that we found was generally rice that had been diverted from Saigon to the Viet Cong. This is the kind of work I did."

The trials ended after our testimony. We headed back to Chicago wondering if we had done any good. Joe had left well before us just shaking his head. He was sure the press would somehow turn our testimony around. Soon after we got back to Chicago, we began to see how the turnaround would work. Muy Ba got a call from the *Chicago Sun Times* while I was at work. She confirmed to the reporter William Schmidt that I had appeared at the war crimes trial. This story then appeared in the Chicago Sun Times on February 3, 1971:

DETROIT---A Chicagoan Lawrence Ryan charged Tuesday that a U.S. Army unit commander in Vietnam inflated an official body count by digging up old graves and counting the corpses as enemy soldiers killed in battle. Ryan, 29, said the officer reported 18 enemy killed in action whereas in reality there was only one.

Ryan said the incident took place after a brief engagement between a 25th Army Division unit and the Viet Cong near Cu Chi, about 20 miles north of Saigon in February or March of 1967. The ex-soldier, now a salesman, appeared at the Winter Soldier Investigation public hearing at a Detroit hotel.

And now for the turnaround that my friend Joe Duffy had predicted. A later edition of the Chicago Sun Times the same day had what appeared to be the same article. The message was totally changed and here it is:

Testifies how Yank officer falsified count of enemy slain

By William Schmidt Special to the Sun Times

DETROIT--A Chicagoan Larry Ryan charged Tuesday that a U.S. Army unit commander in Vietnam counted bodies awaiting burial in a cemetery and added them to an official tally of enemy soldiers killed in combat.

Ryan, age 29, said the incident took place in February or March,1967, after a brief combat engagement between a 25th Army Division unit and the Viet Cong near Cu Chi, about 20 miles north of Saigon.

One Viet Cong was killed in the action, related Ryan, who said he was serving as a Public Information Office enlisted man at the time. He added: He's a salesman.

"As a result, the unit commander counted 16 bodies in a nearby graveyard and counted them as body count. He took credit for 17 (enemy) killed.

Now to sort this out, as you can see from my actual testimony above, I never claimed that the child who was murdered lying face down in the grass a few feet in front of this American unit was a Viet Cong. He was an unarmed child who was dressed in shorts and sandals only. The only movements he made were from breathing. His beautiful brown back went up and down just slightly as he waited for the criminal act of the U.S. Commander who stopped his breathing with a burst from an M16 rifle.

The first rendition said the body count was inflated by digging up old graves and counting the corpses as enemy soldiers killed in battle. In reality the ground in the old cemetery was hard packed and we didn't dig enough to reveal a single bone. So the first story reported had already cleaned up the story enough to sow confusion as to whether or not we were counting old graves, old corpses or Vietnamese soldiers recently killed in battle.

The second rendition finished the pro war propaganda job quoting me as saying that bodies in the cemetery were counted. Now it's time again for three cheers for freedom of the press as long as it gets the story fucked up enough to make Washington happy.

CHAPTER 44

Washington

We watched and read the war news anxiously. Kissinger managed to sabotage the Paris peace talks at every turn. We decided not to just sit around and wait for the war to end. We went to D.C. for the VVAW protest at the nation's capital. We called it a "limited incursion into the country of Congress." I stood in front of the Capitol and cheered as Congressman Ron Dellums of California denounced the war in a speech to the assembled vets. I was out in front of the Capitol when John Kerry testified against the war during Senate Foreign Relations Committee hearings.

At 4:30 that afternoon, at the time the vets were supposed to clear off the Mall as ordered by the Supreme Court, nobody moved. A deal was offered--the vets could stay but only if they stayed awake all night. Several VVAW leaders tried to win vets to this deal. After much debate a vote was taken; by a small majority the vets decided to sleep rather than to take the deal. Another vote was taken, and all the vets voted to go with the majority. The Justice Department backed down. No arrests were made, and the vets won a major victory defying the Supreme Court. That night the vets slept on the Mall.

I said hello to Senator Ted Kennedy who walked in the Mall with our motley contingent of diehard antiwar vets and then went back to Arlington VA where Muy Ba and I were staying with Republican friends who were strongly opposed to the war.

The following day, April 24, 1971 we joined 500,000 war protesters and marched to Congress to lobby against the war. Pete Seeger walked just a few feet in front of us with 200,000 marchers in front of him and 300,000 behind him. As we marched past the FBI building at 935 Pennsylvania AV NW., we sang with him:

"This land is your land, this land is my land
From California, to the New York Island
From the redwood forest, to the gulf stream waters
This land was made for you and me."

Black clerks and secretaries waved at us from the FBI building windows as we sang. The FBI brass was probably cowering in the back wondering how in hell they could arrest us. Had we been facing the Ohio National Guard they may well have simply starting shooting.

Muy Ba and I headed back to Chicago that afternoon. We had the red Plymouth to ourselves and enjoyed the privacy. She was very happy because the antiwar rally and march made her believe the war would end soon.

Back in Chicago Bill Ayers had news for us. Because of the news coverage of the Winter Soldier war crimes trial, antiwar vets were needed to speak at churches all over the area. My first assignment was a small gathering of the Women's Alliance in the basement of a Unitarian church on the west side of Chicago in the Austin neighborhood. The church had had many more members in the past but when the neighborhood became all black, half the members left to start a new church in the nearby suburb of Oak Park. All of the antiwar activists who I met with in the Paul Robeson room were white. Anne, a pretty young woman, introduced me and explained to the audience that it was my first time speaking in public and I had only agreed to answer questions.

"I'll ask the first question to get things started," she said. "Were you worried about getting shot when you arrived in Vietnam?"

I answered easily that "… of course I was. I was supposed to be wearing olive green underwear but had not bothered to mess up my last days at home coloring clothes so as I sat on a cot that first evening in my white T-shirt assuming I'd be easy to spot by some nearby Viet Cong."

Another young woman said, "I wonder what it was like trying to win the hearts and minds of the Vietnamese as you walked around armed to the teeth?"

"Winning their hearts was a cruel joke," I answered." We burned their villages, raped their women and passed out candy bars to weeping children."

The next questioner wondered about the recruiting practice of not so subtly offering sex as an incentive to our eighteen-year olds. I told about the R&R's that were offered which took our teenagers to brothels in Thailand and all-over Southeast Asia. These antiwar folks were saddened to hear that so many of our young men did not even get a single R&R because of the horrendous number of casualties in the infantry units.

Anne wondered if I had any firsthand experience with such adventures. I admitted to taking five R&R's and hinted at the pleasures of the massage with three girls in Bangkok. Anne wanted more information. I asked if she was sure this kind of talk was appropriate in the Church basement.

"Just give us one more example," she said. So I proceeded to tell about my favorite hangout in Saigon, The Saigon Health Club Massage No Sex. When I was almost to the volcano eruption part Anne said, "OK that about does it for this part of the program. Shirley will now give the treasurer's report and discuss plans for the Mother/ Daughter banquet."

There were complaints from the audience about Anne cutting me off, but she ignored them and volunteered to walk me to the train. Just as we headed north towards Paul Robson Way, the power went out. We then walked streets gloriously devoid of city lights.

"I didn't realize Chicago had stars! Just look."

She took my hand and we circled back towards the now candlelit church. There was a playroom for religious education in the rear of the building. She opened the door and led me into the darkened space. We stumbled onto a couch and she fell into my arms and said, "Now tell me about the volcano." She kissed me somewhat aggressively and placed my free hand on her breast.

"Sorry," I said, "But if we don't loosen your bra I'm afraid your nipples will damage it."

She laughed then said, "We had better be quiet or the whole crowd will come back to investigate."

Once I got a taste of her silky thighs, I was a goner.

When I got home, I worried that Muy Ba would be asking for kisses, but she was busy reading mail that had come from Hanoi via the good Doctor. I took *For Whom the Bell Tolls*, by Hemingway to the bathroom. As I filled the tub while sitting on the toilet, I tried to read the book in Spanish.

After the bath with my guilt going down the drain, I went to bed with the book.

CHAPTER 45

On the Road Again

An opportunity came along for me to do sales work for a medical supply company and I took it. The company was called Castle. It was based in Rochester New York. I hated the thought of giving up the red Plymouth but looked forward to the new Chevy Impala that Castle offered. The job was a new position with the company selling hospital equipment through medical supply dealers. The country was divided into quarters and I was assigned twelve Midwestern states. I went to the home office in New York for a week of training which pretty much flew over my head. I was sent home to study the binders full of product literature the pleasant boss, Bill, had provided and told to wait for my company car which would be ready soon.

While waiting for the car Muy Ba and I went to dinner at the Berghoff Restaurant in the Chicago Loop. I had the house beer on tap and Muy Ba had a draft root beer in a big frosty mug. We both ordered the wiener schnitzel which was the special. It came with coleslaw and hot German potato salad.

Muy Ba took a bite of the schnitzel and said, "yum yum." It was veal that had been sliced thin, tenderized, breaded and deep fried. I loved it and said, "We should come here more often."

"I didn't think the Germans people could cook so good like Julia Childs."

We were spending the expense advance that the new boss had given me. We talked about the extensive travel that would be required and planned to do the work together. We went to St Louis, Detroit, Kansas City and Minneapolis all in the first month. Muy Ba stayed in the various hotel rooms and read while I wined and dined the new customers.

While in Detroit we saw a sign that said tunnel to Canada, so we drove right under the Detroit River and told the customs agent we weren't carrying guns or commercial goods. She sent us to the side anyway. I had answered, "Gary, Indiana," when the immigration agent asked where I was born. Muy Ba answered by saying, "Hanoi, can't you tell?" We were waved through for some strange reason. I was clearly not the only one who couldn't resist the adorable little Commie.

We walked the European-like Ouellette Avenue in downtown Windsor and stopped for dinner at a fine fish joint. After dinner we walked down the Avenue to the beautiful Dieppe Gardens. The view through the Gardens and across the Detroit River was stunning.

I had escaped the church basement liaison without a scratch, but guilt still kept me awake worrying that my slam bam tastes were returning and would ruin my wonderful marriage.

While out on the road alone working for Castle Company, I managed to eat fish, drink white wine and go to bed early. Muy Ba always jumped up and down when I walked up the front stairs of our house on Seminary Avenue carrying my little brown briefcase stuffed with sterilizer specifications that made no sense to me.

One lovely evening, sitting on the bench on our front porch at the Seminary house, we talked about going back to the Berghoff but settled for a New York strip steak grilled to perfection on the Weber grill with the white wall tires. Muy Ba was worried that her sauce Bearnaise came out a little lumpy, but it was delicious just the same.

In the morning Muy Ba headed to school on the L train and I went to work in the backyard trying to grow tomatoes in the cinder filled plot. I hung my garden rake on the chain link fence that I had installed upside down illegally but accidently. Luckily no kids ever got injured jumping over the fence.

Noting my cinder filled plight the lovely young newlywed from next door stopped by with a cute little brown puppy. She was still short of underwear, it seemed, because her fine stiff nipples were right there tickling my tender balls-eyeballs that is. I reached for the puppy and as the back of my hand slid down the doggy fur, she pulled the pup to her trapping my happy hand. Caught between a soft puppy and a stiff nipple!

"Come on upstairs to my place and look at my wedding pictures," she said conspiratorially. No one saw us enter her place through the back door and we were soon on our hands and knees in her sparsely furnished living room. She had managed to loosen two buttons on her blouse and I found myself mesmerized staring at her tits as she went hurriedly through the photos that meant nothing to me and even less to her I suspected. We stood and pointing at her bed in the next room she said, "Look at the mess my husband has made on the sheets with his greasy head. He comes home from work at the gas station at seven or eight, eats dinner and goes to bed exhausted and without showering. He hasn't even kissed me since the first week. Now I don't even want him to. Will you help me put clean sheets on the bed?" she purred.

As we stretched the fitted sheet in place she said, "Look at that spot that didn't come out even though I scrubbed on it by hand." She didn't like how I was pulling on the top sheet and came around the bed to help. "Like this," she said as she pulled my arm across her glorious nipples.

"Give me a little hug before I cry," she begged.

The clean sheets were delightful, and with my mouth full of young tit I realized that I had a problem and didn't care. Too much pussy is not a disease, it's an impossibility.

Later I went to the fish market on Randolph Street and bought a Lake Superior whitefish filet that was taken from a tub being prepared for restaurant delivery. I had Julia Child on the table when Muy Ba got home from school and told her I was looking for a recipe for the fish. She said, "Go sit down Larry and pour me a glass of wine. We need to celebrate."

"Fine," I said. "So, what are we celebrating?"

She lifted her glass of Chardonnay and toasted," Larry and Muy Ba--already happy married one whole year."

The wine was not that cheap, but it seemed bitter.

After dinner Muy Ba tried to hug and kiss but I turned away because of my guilt.

"Why don't you want to kiss me anymore?" she said.

"I'm just tired," I said.

She started crying and said, "I came home early from school today and went upstairs to talk with Esmeralda since you weren't home. I was looking out the window through her sheer curtains when you came sneaking down the back stairs from that dirty white slut's apartment.

"She's not a slut. She was just showing me her wedding pictures."

"So then why didn't you want to kiss your pretty brown wife? And why don't you ever want to kiss me when you come home from talking to those ugly white ladies about the war?"

I went into the bedroom and closed the door and started to cry. I knew this day would come but was still not ready for it. Muy Ba came into the room and sat on the bed beside me, "You are such a stupid white G.I. You go with those ugly nigger gook white fuck ladies then come home to make me sick."

I wondered if she would ever call me silly again. I certainly didn't deserve it.

"Doctor LeDuc wants me to meet a nice young Vietnamese man who works for him. He says it will be easy for me to a get a divorce from you because you go with so many other ladies. He says I could marry that boy and then go back to Hanoi when the war is over and help build the new country."

I just rolled over and continued crying as she left the room. I looked at the wall that no longer had a window because we had drywalled over it for privacy. When there was still a curtain there, I had taken a picture of Muy Ba standing there with the afternoon sun filtering through a sheer curtain. She was nude and the light on her small brown body magically took me back to Can Duoc where I had first seen her nude as she bathed in the clear pool beside the path that went from the pineapple boat to the village. The thought of losing her now was more than I could handle. The weeping became wailing then went back to weeping and continued until I finally went to sleep.

CHAPTER 46

Treatment

I was up early the next morning and felt pretty good considering the circumstances. Muy Ba was already gone to see Dr. Le Chan. I was sure she would be back, so I fixed myself a bowl of cold cereal topped with a sliced, barely ripe banana. When she returned a couple of hours later, I had finished some customer calls and was reading the *New York Times* while drinking black coffee.

She was surprised to see me looking so normal. "Why aren't you still crying, you crazy sick G.I.?"

"I'm not a G.I. anymore thank gods, but I can't argue about the crazy part. I would also add stupid and degenerate. Did you share our catastrophe with the good doctor?"

"Yes, and I told him that I have decided to get divorce from you and go back Vietnam. He said it would be easy to get divorce under the circumstances but he just pick up his ugly old black telephone and call doctor friend of his at the Veterans Administration Hospital. With me sitting right in front of him feeling like little lost girl without map he told the other doctor all about us."

"Did he tell the other doctor about our antiwar work?"

"No, but the other doctor is also Vietnamese and would probably be very happy to hear that you are not all bad. He tell Doctor Le Chan that you are a sick soldier. He said many soldiers come home messed up like you. He said VA has medicine for these sick soldiers and many of them can be cured. Then the other doctor asked about illegal drugs and alcohol so Doctor Le Chan put his hand over phone and asked me if you drunken often and if you were addicted to drugs. I told him that you sold some bad drugs like those you used to stay awake to drive to Acapulco but not often. He asked again about the drunken and I said we like to drink a little wine together. Then I just cried."

"Then what happened?"

"He asked if I still wanted divorce or to try treatment. I said I know I want to get divorce and go home to my family in Vietnam. Then he looked very sad just like me and said I needed to ask you about treatment."

"I hope you want me to try the treatment."

"Do you want me or the stinking white whore ladies?"

"I only want you, Muy Ba, and I hope you want me to go see the new doctor."

She gave me a card that said:

Mental Health
West Side Veterans Administration Hospital
Doctor Murry
312-525-7991

I dialed the number and was told that if this was an emergency I should hang up and dial 911 so I hung up. Muy Ba asked what happened and I told her. She made me call right back and called me silly. She saw me look at her and quickly corrected that to stupid.

I had previously been in the hospital for 10 days for treatment of an infection I had apparently brought home from Vietnam. They thought it might be *Neisseria gonorrhoeae,* but it was not positively identified so I was given Keflin IV. The strong broad-spectrum drug seemed to do the trick. Because of that hospital stay it was easy to set up an appointment with the new doctor in the hospital's mental health clinic.

There were signs everywhere:

1-800-273-TALK (8255)
Press 1 for Veterans
It takes the strength and courage of a warrior to ask for help...
Emotional Crisis? Call 1-800-272-talk(8255).
Nurse Advice Line
24 hours a day/7 days a week
Call 1-800-4596610 [Toll free]
Stand by Them
The Veterans Crisis Line Is Here For You
Confidential help for Veterans and their families
Veterans Crisis Line

To get to the clinic I had to walk that surreal gauntlet of suicide warnings. I hadn't heard that too much pussy caused suicide, but who can say?

I finally reached the desk in the mental health clinic and was greeted with a friendly smile by Heather but then whamo, she handed me a keychain that read "If someone you know is in an emotional crisis…"

She pleasantly asked for my name and last four, which is the VA's way of asking for the last four digits of your Social Security number.

Soon I was seated in Doctor Murray's office answering questions.

"Have you ever considered suicide?"

No kidding! That was the very first question. I didn't want to make trouble, so I just answered but I had to wonder if he had bothered to look at my folder.

I said, "No."

"Have any close friends or family committed suicide?"

"No, but my brother attempted it when he was sixteen."

"Why do you think he tried and how did he do it?"

So, I told him about getting called home from college by our pastor and showing up at Mercy Hospital in downtown Gary, Indiana. My baby brother Tim was still out from the anesthesia for the surgery that had been done to put his torn liver back together. He had shot himself with a 22 rifle but had missed the heart he was aiming for.

The VA doctor repeated the question about why I thought my brother had done it. So, I told him about my parent's child rearing techniques which were church at least four times a week and excessive prayer every day. When that failed the belt would come out and he would be beaten for a few minutes. I said that it was just this sort of insanity that caused my older brother to bail out as soon as he could get into the Marines at age 17.

Tim was an adorable baby and a fun-loving toddler. The neighbors and everyone else loved him. The neighbors to the south would hire him to go to the grocery store for milk and bread. He was so proud of the shiny quarters he would earn. But whatever he did was never enough for Mom. "Why can't you memorize Bible verses like Larry? Why don't you get ready for Sunday School on time like Larry?"

When school started it was "Why can't you get good grades like Larry?"

I was the goody goody who never swore and made it into Wheaton College while he struggled with reading and writing and dropped out as soon as he hit sixteen. Neither brother nor my Dad managed to finish 10th grade.

"Do you feel guilty about your role in his attempted suicide?" he asked.

"Of course!" I answered. I loved my role as the good son. I then told him that I had apologized to both brothers for being so shitty.

"And now I see from reading your folder you have pretty much gotten over your good boy role."

"Yes, a good war'll do that to a person."

"So, you blame the war for your problems?"

"Well for sure I would be a totally different person if I had not gone to Vietnam."

"Would you like to turn the clock back if you could?"

"Right now, a lot of things are going through my mind that I would like to do over."

"Do you want to tell me about them?"

"Hell no!"

"Why?"

"I don't want to get kicked out my first visit. I did come here for help, not to get criticized for the mistakes I've made even though I agree I've made plenty. If you think

I'm just blaming the Army for my imperfections, I think I should say thanks anyway and leave."

"I will not criticize you for anything. We are trained to not be judgmental. If we tried to work any other way, nobody would come back for a second visit. Would you at least like to say something about the sex issues that prompted you to come here?"

"I thought that you would know from my folder that my wife was going to leave me and go back to Hanoi if I didn't sign up for treatment."

"Yes' I saw that, but we need to start someplace if we are going to be successful in finding treatment for you."

"Do you mean drugs?"

"Well I'm a medical doctor with a closet full of drugs," he said as he pointed to a large, gray, double doored metal cabinet across the room. "But before we can talk about a treatment plan, I need to find out more about you. So, let's start at the beginning. What are some of these sex issues?"

I decided to start with my first visit to the *Saigon Health Club Massage no Sex*. He stuck with me as I paid my $5 in Vietnamese Dong and was aroused by the lovely Ba Muy walking on my bare ass. As soon as it became obvious where the story was headed, he looked at his watch and said, "I think it would be best for you to give this history to one of our social workers."

He picked up the phone and asked for Isabella. "I'm talking with a new patient, Larry Ryan, and would like for you to meet with him as soon as possible to hear his story about what sounds to me like a possible sex addiction problem."

So much for being non-judgmental I thought.

"She can see you anytime Tuesday afternoon next week, will that be OK?"

I said it would be and he said perfunctorily that he was happy to have met me and we would talk about a treatment plan as soon as I finished with Isabella. He told me to stop at the desk and have Heather make the appointment.

Muy Ba was pleased to hear that I had made it to my appointment and would be going back to meet Isabella again Tuesday afternoon.

Tuesday rolled around and I was a few minutes early. I gave Heather my last four and was told to take a seat. I sat next to an attractive young brunette named Delores who was tending her toddler and waiting for her husband who was in with Doctor Murray. Across from us a young couple argued about what to do with their obnoxious five-year-old.

Suddenly the trunk of a person wheeled himself out into the lobby. He was flat on his stomach on what auto mechanics call a car creeper. He smiled as he looked up at Dolores and she started to smile back when her obnoxious five-year-old yelled, "Look, Mommy, a real monster."

The man on the creeper was Captain Jack Olson. His tank had been blown up by a massive anti-tank mine during fighting around Nui Ba Den (known as Black Virgin Mountain by the Americans) in a May 1968 battle. Many Americans died in the battle. He survived because a heroic medic kept him alive until the battle ended then rode with him on a medevac chopper to a field hospital where his shredded arms and legs had to be removed. The medic died in another battle soon after. Captain Olson sends the medic's widow a check every month.

Dolores and her broken family were about to flee through the automatic door as if nothing had happened when Captain Olson said, "It's good to be called a monster for a change. It makes me feel more human. The well-intentioned syrupy sympathy I usually get is depressing."

Dolores then introduced herself to the Captain and thanked him for his kind words.

"Would you be willing to bring Joey up to my monster lair on the fifth floor?" I think he'll be impressed with the experimental gadgetry the VA has loaded my room with.

I sat there in tears wondering why I should be taking up space at the VA when others needed care far more than me. The Captain surprised me by saying in a strong voice, "Come along with us Larry, I have a super cool suite and I love to show it off."

Why not? I thought so up we all went.

The first one to speak as we entered the Captain's extraordinary room was Dolores. She said, "You sure were handsome before your tragedy."

The good Captain had tricked her. All the photos were recent.

"How can that be?" a shocked Dolores said.

"They are publicity shots for my public appearances and videos."

"So, you can walk? asked Joey.

"No, I can't take a single step or even stand without support."

"What kind of videos?" I asked.

"Mostly to promote my line of gadgets that I brought you up here to see."

The Captain moved to the side of his bed and tapped a button with the stylus that was the end of his right arm stub.

His bed seemed to be doing a somersault as it rotated, grabbed him and left him in an upright position with his head at eye level with me.

"Have a seat Joey." he said.

Joey sat and the Captain brought him up to level with the rest of us.

"Cool", Joey said, "You are now officially my favorite monster."

"But you ain't seen nothin' yet kid!"

"Now what?" I said excitedly.

"To run my business, I need to do a lot of writing and I don't always want somebody in the room with me to take dictation and I don't work well with a recorder. So, when I wake up at two in the morning and want to work, I just push this button and *voila,* I'm off to the races."

All of the panels flipped and were replaced by thousands of words and numbered phrases that were printed on the back of the panels. The Captain gave us a demo using the stylus to incorporate numbered phrases into his text and using shorthand as well.

"What do you mean business?" Dolores asked.

"Any idea I come up with that helps me will also help other amputees, and believe me, there are more of them than you can imagine."

"Why are there so many?" I asked just so Dolores and Joey would hear the answer.

"The most obvious answer is war, since we are here in this fine VA hospital where injured veterans are given the best care available, including prosthetics, physical therapy and voice activated assistance.

However, most of my business comes from traffic accidents. Since we don't have decent public transportation, when folks party they often end up driving home drunk. They don't always make it. The sad thing is the young people usually crash simply because they are inexperienced drivers. So, Joey, I suggest you learn how to drive before you drink. Or move to a country where the drunks pass out on the buses and trains on the way home.

The rich kids who lose their limbs don't get much government help and certainly no free prosthetics, so Daddy comes to the rescue. And he comes to see me. And I make a killing!"

Joey seemed to zone out staring at the panel showing the service dogs while the Captain talked about drinking and driving.

"What about the puppy dogs?", Joey asked.

"The kennel is in a barn outside the hospital. It currently has maybe twenty golden retriever pups and fifteen German Shepherd puppies. The vets who are in need of service dogs go to the barn everyday as part of their rehab and the puppies are responsible for choosing their new masters. The program is run by a veterinarian, Doctor Charlene Mitchell, who wrote the book on service dog placement."

"Why don't you have doctor Murray come here to your fine office? "I asked.

"He has been here, but he generally prefers to have me go to his office for business matters. Today I had a contract for him to sign. I have hired him to do consulting for my business. We made a video a while back which was mostly just a question and answer session about veterans dealing with depression, ego and personal relationships. "The video was a big hit with amputees."

Joey pretty much ended our meeting with the Captain by thanking him and saying, "You almost make me wish I were an amputee and I sure don't think you're a monster anymore."

When I got back to Isabella's office a few minutes later she said," All right, let's get started. I've read your record and see why Doctor Murray sent you to me. He seems to think social workers are much better at sex talk and sex listening than psychiatrists."

"Well I hope so. He sure wasn't about to take the time to understand my issues."

"That's no doubt why we work together. So, I see you got as far as this girl walking on your bare ass before Murray panicked. Do you want to tell me what happened next?"

She bent over to pick up a piece of lint. It was obvious that she was attractive and as I looked down her blouse, I thought "Oh no, here we go again." But of course, that was not to be.

"So, what happened?" she asked, and I told her.

Isabella walked me through several of my wartime encounters with willing women and girls then looked at the clock and said, "Time's up unfortunately. That was probably the quickest hour ever here for me. Please stop at the desk and make another appointment so that we can continue the Larry Ryan Gone Amuck Story."

She smiled as she said "amuck," so I thanked her and left without so much as a handshake or a hug.

Isabella stuck with me for several weeks listening cheerfully to all the gory details. Finally sounding a bit disappointed she said, "Dr Murray wonders if we are ready to talk about a treatment plan."

I said, "I don't exactly crave the medical doctor's drugs."

She said, "I think I can help you. Should I tell him you prefer to spend more time with me?"

I managed to restrain myself and said nothing about wanting to spend the night with her and just said, "Yes, please do."

Isabella had mechanical techniques in mind to help me get on with my newly acquired monogamous ways. The first thing on her list was, "No more out of town travel for business."

There would be no more visits to the buy one get one girl free at the Express Body Wash in Sioux City Iowa. I had promised to just ask for the lovely free girl next time, but Isabella was adamant.

That meant getting another new job. The same headhunter that put me on the road for Castle Company understood the problem and soon had me working a Chicago area sales territory for Baxter Labs.

Isabella then asked, "What are we going to do about the church ladies with the hard nipples?"

I said, "Are you serious? Why of course we will pray for them."

"Seriously, you can now only take speaking engagements when Muy Ba or Doctor Le Chan are willing to go with you."

"So, I'm to be chaperoned?"

"Do you have a better idea?"

I sat there, tongue tied to my foot, for the rest of the session, then said as I stood to leave, "I do love Muy Ba more than anything else in the world and will definitely give it a try."

With the new regime in place my homelife slowly came back to the heaven I knew was best. We went every place together. My speeches to peace groups around the city now lacked the electricity of imminent sex but Muy Ba really came into her own as a public speaker. At first, I would ask her to help me answer questions but soon the word got out that she could hold her own even with a large audience.

It had to happen. An urgent request came for Muy Ba to fill in at a major event for the scheduled speaker who had to cancel at the last minute.

She accepted and this time I was her chaperone. As we walked to the podium heads turned because of her stunning beauty which was highlighted by a spectacular silk *ao dai* that had arrived recently from Hanoi via a friend of the general's in Paris.

As she worked her way convincingly through her youth in Hanoi to falling in love with Larry Ryan on the pineapple boat, the audience stopped staring and hung on to every heartfelt word.

She brought the house down and they were all on their feet applauding and screaming as she walked back to her seat with me in tow.

The organizers decided to skip the next speaker and jumped straight to Reverend Jesse Jackson who was the movement's number one shakedown artist at the time. He badgered and cajoled, calling out one especially dapper black pastor with, "I see you hiding behind your lovely wife back there Reverend Jeremiah. You heard Muy Ba speak. Money is needed to keep her on the road telling the truth about this unholy war. I saw you pull up in that big old boat of a Cadillac. Make it a thousand now before I'm forced to tell the world about…"

More than double the amount of money hoped for poured into the baskets that were circulated by the dynamite Chicago Black Baptist Choir as they sang: *"Precious Lord take my hand, lead me on, let me stand,"* while dancing around the huge auditorium.

CHAPTER 47

Silky White Temptation

My cousin Wally Morris was killed in Vietnam soon after I had returned in July 1967. Aunt Florence can now visit her first-born son in Washington, D.C., and perhaps use a pencil to rub his name and date of death on to a piece of paper. I have done that for Wally and my three friends, Jimmy, Joe and Dave who died on April 10th, 1967, just 20 feet from me.

Wally's last two letters home told of being wounded. Each time he said the wounds were not serious and he would be back in the field with his unit soon. It had sounded like that was where he wanted to be.

Muy Ba and I were enjoying the front porch just waiting for mail from Hanoi when the phone rang. It was my Mom with the sad news. My cousin Wally was her oldest nephew.

The funeral was scheduled for Saturday. We had a speaking engagement at the same time at the same Westside church where the same nice lady with the bra-busting nipples would again run the program. Muy Ba and Doctor John, that's what he wanted us to call him, decided to handle the church commitment and said I would have to go alone back to Indiana for the funeral.

Driving out to Hobart alone for the service gave me too much time to think about all the fun I had had playing with Wally over the years. His house was near Ridge Road just a little East of Gary. Big brother Jim and I had once found matches in the basement of the house and took them out for a smoking adventure. We picked up butts along the road and smoked them. I remember laying on Aunt Florence's couch looking out the window in nauseous agony. I never smoked again!

Big brother was much older at the time, maybe ten, and just got hooked. The addiction would eventually kill him. We learned from his oldest son Rob after he died that he had never really stopped smoking even though he had convinced his wife, who never smoked, that he had.

I was angered and appalled at the funeral service. It was stage managed by the American Legion. The closed coffin was draped with the American flag. I stood rigid like an old stump looking north to the orange sky that always hung over Gary when the mills were pumping out smoke and steam from the plate mill where my Dad worked. The coke, high carbon fuel made by super-heating coal without oxygen, was used to fire the blast furnaces that warmed the steel so that it could be rolled into plates of various thicknesses depending on the customer's needs.

An honor guard fired into the air. Dirt was thrown into the grave. When the short shovel with the sweaty handle was passed to me and the music got to "bombs bursting in air," I started to cry. Then my mother cried and soon everyone was bawling.

Someone took my hand and I assumed it was my mother. When she held me close, I smelled a pleasant perfume and realized it was my old white girlfriend, Nancy. My heart ached as I thought about how crazy I had been to leave her and go to war.

The crowd at the moment was tearfully antiwar despite the Legion's best intentions. Mourners began to slowly fade back to their cars parked nearby under the lovely red and black oak trees.

The busy squirrels provided a proper funeral dirge bouncing acorns off the cars as Nancy continued to comfort me and told me that her marriage hadn't worked out. She wanted me to stop by her place on the way back to Chicago.

I thought about devouring her wonderful tits while parked in my little red MGA in her driveway just three years ago. Back then luckily, or unfortunately, her father had come to the porch door and called for her to come in.

I thanked her rather bluntly for coming to the funeral but declined her current offer for more comfort. I started driving back to Muy Ba alone wracked by emotion.

Isabella at the VA had told me that it was important to break the habit of promiscuity and that once broken life would be easier.

As I drove, I identified with St. Paul on the road to Damascus, Syria. I realized that I had had my very own epiphany and would meet the challenges to our successful marriage in the days and years ahead.

Larry Ryan and Muy Ba lived happily ever after. In 1996, after the U.S. and Vietnam resumed diplomatic relations they even went to Hanoi to announce to her parents that they were soon to be grandparents.

THE END

EPILOGUE

Five years later Muy Ba and Larry went back to Hanoi for the funeral of her father, General Giap. They walked in the Hoan Kiem Lake Park across from where Muy Ba had grown up. Doctor Le Chan had flown over with them to say farewell to his friend and commander. He held Madame Giap's arm as they reminisced.

Bill Ayers and Bernardine Dohrn were removed from the FBI's most wanted list and Bill was thriving as a writing professor at the University of Illinois while Bernardine served less than a year in prison after turning herself in to the authorities. She has been a clinical law professor at Northwestern University.

Jerry, Sally and Emmett did just fine in Chicago where they stayed not far from Lake Michigan where they enjoyed sailing. Judy and Suzy sold the bookstore in San Francisco, graduated from seminary and took a position co-pastoring a large Unitarian church in Kansas City, Missouri.

ABOUT THE AUTHOR

Larry Craig, frequent NYTimes.com commen-tator, was raised in Gary, Indiana, and attended Calumet High School. He joined the Army hoping to help save the Vietnamese from godless communism, but six months into his fifteen-month tour realized we were supporting the wrong side in a civil war. He earned a master's degree in education from Governors State University in Illinois and taught first grade before becoming a sales and marketing executive. He retired from Siemens Medical Systems in 1996.

I wrote this book hoping to bury the demons that kept me awake most nights for many years. In 1967 I witnessed the murder of a child near Tay Ninh, Vietnam. Chapter one in this book is an enhanced account of the incident. The writing therapy which had been recom-mended by a Veterans Administration social worker worked. I now sleep better than most babies.

Made in the USA
Monee, IL
01 March 2021